D1323042

THE ODYSSEY

Withdrawn From Stock
Dublin City Public Libraries

By the same author

Supper Club
Treats

THE ODYSSEY

Lara Williams

HAMISH HAMILTON
an imprint of
PENGUIN BOOKS

HAMISH HAMILTON

UK | USA | Canada | Ireland | Australia
India | New Zealand | South Africa

Hamish Hamilton is part of the Penguin Random House group of companies
whose addresses can be found at global.penguinrandomhouse.com.

First published 2022
001

Copyright © Lara Williams, 2022

The moral right of the author has been asserted

Waves design by Amelia Stewart from the Noun Project

Set in 12.25/15 pt Fournier MT Std
Typeset by Jouve (UK), Milton Keynes
Printed and bound in Great Britain by Clays Ltd, Elcograf S.p.A.

The authorized representative in the EEA is Penguin Random House Ireland,
Morrison Chambers, 32 Nassau Street, Dublin D02 YH68

A CIP catalogue record for this book is available from the British Library

ISBN: 978–0–241–50281–5

www.greenpenguin.co.uk

MIX
Paper from
responsible sources
FSC® C018179

Penguin Random House is committed to a
sustainable future for our business, our readers
and our planet. This book is made from Forest
Stewardship Council® certified paper.

For Marek and Peet

Land

What you need to understand, Keith said, *is that everything is coming out of and going into nothingness. That is the principle of wabi sabi.*

He gestured around his office. Shelves lined with glass figurines and ornamental vases. Jewelled pillboxes and self-conscious curios. He reached over to pick up a grey clay pot from his desk. *You see*, he said, running his thumb over a small chip at the rim. *Do you see?*

I nodded.

Now you try, he said.

I looked around the room. It was the first time I had met him. It was hard to know how to behave. I pointed to an oil painting. Fruit in a bowl. *Is that wabi sabi?* I asked.

No, he replied, shaking his head.

I pointed to a paperweight. A smooth silver ball. *Is that wabi sabi?* I asked.

No, he replied.

I pointed to a vase on one of the filing cabinets. Earth-brown and gently lopsided. *Is that wabi sabi?* I asked.

Now you're getting it, he replied, snapping his fingers.

Leabharlann Peambróg
Pembroke Library
01-2228450

Sea

I got the memo while on rotation in the gift shop. I liked working at the gift shop and I particularly liked working the cash register. It was positioned in the middle of the shop, a single column of heavy wood. It felt like I was sailing the ship. I'd rest my elbows against it while surveying the space, breathing stale, recycled air. I'd watch customers move lethargically between the aisles and pretend I was in charge of them all, issuing instructions in my head. Sometimes they would obey my instructions and I would get a very warm feeling, the kind of feeling I used to get from watching a video of a dog on the internet. It would sustain me for a little while.

From the register I could see almost everything in the store. To my right were the artisanal and novelty chocolates. Flavours like wasabi and goat curd, gouda and sun-dried tomatoes. Beside them were the edible insects, exoskeletons dipped in dark chocolate or salted caramel. To my left were the animal-skin rugs and blankets, all different kinds, all perfectly intact. The skin slipped from the body the way athletic girls can peel an apple in a single, flawless spiral. At the front of the shop were racks of allegedly designer clothes, with brand names I had never heard of, though they all sounded European enough to be convincing.

Further afield were perfumes and cosmetics, vodka in skull-shaped glass bottles and clocks made from old records, earrings cut out from bits of Lego and pens capped with real gold, watches that would work five hundred feet beneath the ocean's surface. There were cheaper things as well. Plastic key rings and T-shirts with the *WA* logo and

Leabharlanna Poiblí Chathair Baile Átha Cliath
Dublin City Public Libraries

coffee cups that said *I Love You, Mum*. There was an operatic quality to it. A domed roof and heavy velvet curtains. A white marble-effect floor threaded with veins of gold and grey. The air smelled oily and perfumed. The day before, an American couple came in and the woman looked around the shop and said, *Honey, isn't this great, we can buy all our presents without ever having to leave the boat*. It was one of many identical gift shops on board.

I'd begun my morning by mopping the floors, which was also my last job of the day. If I worked the late shift followed by the early shift I would get this unpleasant feeling of hovering in and out of myself, like my body and brain couldn't agree on where I was standing in the order of time. I'd often have to retrace my steps, waking up and then falling asleep and then going to bed and then taking off my make-up. Sometimes I'd have to go further back, remembering when I started working on the ship, when I left my old apartment, when I got married, when I passed my entrance exams, when I broke my arm roller-skating. Recently I'd developed this compulsion where I would try to figure out what I was doing exactly a year earlier, but it was hard work after several years on the *WA*. I had done the same things so many times. Mia would call this my *auto chronological endo pathology*. She could be pretty smart when she wasn't pretending to be a baby.

After I mopped the floor I wiped down the surfaces and sprayed the room with very expensive air freshener. I removed the fresh flowers from the fresh-flower fridge and arranged them around the shop. I was the only staff member on rotation trained in arranging the fresh flowers. This is something my co-worker, Zach, hated me for. He told me I was not a visual person. He told me that at least twice a day. Often, after I had finished arranging the flowers, he'd go over to them and act as though he was plucking invisible pieces of fluff from them, but he would never actually touch them, because he knew he was not allowed to. I watched him do this from the register, rolling my eyes and hoping he'd notice.

Mid-morning, I watched a customer pick up a rhinestone-studded T-shirt spelling *Chic*, holding it against her body and watching herself in the mirror. Buy it! I thought. Buy it! Buy it! But she did not, returning it to its slim glass shelf, folded inexpertly but not inexpertly enough that I felt compelled to fix it. I felt my serotonin levels deplete.

By late afternoon the daily newsletter had been delivered. It was filled, as usual, with all the stupid stuff happening on board. A hypnotist in the cocktail lounge. Polynesian night and poke. A talk with a marine biologist in which she was contractually obliged not to answer questions about the sea levels or the dying molluscs or the coral outcrops or the whales.

It also contained what was tenuously labelled *news about the passengers*. A ruby wedding anniversary plus a photograph of the couple holding champagne flutes. So-and-so dying. I imagined Mia walking around the ship and searching for stories. She was on rotation at the news desk. She hated it. She said the only story people had was that they were rich and unhappy.

After we'd finished reading the newsletter we got ready for what we were supposed to refer to as Twilight, the early-evening hours in which we played yé-yé and served French Martinis. Customers would pop by to do some shopping before their evening meal. Many of the female passengers bought gowns or catsuits or new blouses to wear straight out of the store and into dinner. I was often put on changing-room duty because I was good at wrangling zips and making small talk with husbands. I had a good idea of what husbands wanted generally, and I was happy enough to give it to them. But before I could take up my usual position, a courier appeared in the shop entrance, walking towards me holding the envelope out in front of him. It was a plain brown envelope, very humble.

Ingrid, he said. *Are you Ingrid?*

I am, I replied.

Congratulations, he told me. *You have a memo from Keith.*

He handed me the envelope. I held it to my nose and inhaled. It smelled like butter and malt. It smelled like a cake missing a crucial ingredient. My heart moved quickly in my chest. Zach appeared by my side.

Open it, he said.

I stared at him. *Come on*, he said. *We've not got all day.*

I slid my finger beneath the fold and ripped. My hands were shaking slightly. I held the letter in front of my face, noticed the *WA* letterhead, the looping italics of Keith's signature. I ran my thumb over it to confirm it was real and not a scan. I read the text in erratic chunks, like eating a meal the wrong way round. But I already knew what it meant. I knew as soon as I saw the brown envelope.

I've been chosen, I said.

I passed the memo to Zach and pretended to be surprised, like I wanted him to confirm it was true. But really I wanted him to see for himself, to rub it in his face. Zach twisted the head of the anglepoise lamp, spotlighting the paper. I watched his eyes move across it in mechanical lines. He handed it back to me with a taut look of regret.

You've got to be kidding me, he said.

I'm in, I said. *Aren't I?*

You're in, he said. *Fuck sake.*

He tugged the letter back.

What do I do now? I asked.

Clearly, you say yes.

OK. Right. Who do I say yes to?

To Keith. At the ceremony.

Zach was regarding me with a nervous urgency. It was exhausting to witness.

When is the ceremony? I asked.

How can you not know this? Why did you even apply? His face stiffened. *Tomorrow*, he said. *Most likely.*

I looked up at the passengers moving around the shop. The women's gowns grazed the floor, collecting dust. The men wore monochrome, big square shoulders. They were ready to begin their evening. I put the letter in my pocket and told Zach I was leaving. I don't know why. He was not senior to me and I didn't owe him anything.

I've finished my shift, I said.

You've finished more than your shift, he replied.

What's that supposed to mean?

Zach brushed the keys of the register, pretended to be very engaged in the task.

I think you know exactly what I mean, he mumbled, not looking up.

Walking away, I wondered what it was about Zach that I found so offensive. Whether it was how overly tactile he was with the till and its contents. Sometimes I'd catch him running his fingertips over the surface of the fake cruise money some of the customers preferred to shop with. He once told me the money had been designed by Keith himself, and that there were all sorts of hidden meanings in the artwork. The tiger, for example, symbolized power. I glanced back and saw he was watching me leave, his pale eyes freakish and crazed. I quickened my pace towards the exit, feeling like a balloon floating in the sky or an animal wriggled out of its chain, something untethered and set free.

~~~~~

After a shift I'd invariably head straight back to my cabin. The walk took me about half an hour if I didn't use any of the lifts or escalators or walkways. This was quite an average commute. When I first started I was excited by it, the number of different lives you could live all contained within one moving place. You could eat at countless restaurants. You could swim in many pools, each one unique in shape, depth, temperature and concept. You could play mini-golf or try zip-lining or escape from an escape room of which there were several themes. You could flip fake coins into an ornamental pond, scale a vertical garden. There was a newspaper and TV studio. There was a philharmonic concert hall. There was a hospital.

While the kaleidoscopic array of objectively pleasurable options was what drew me to the *WA*, within a year I found I'd mostly just sit in my cabin, occasionally making uninventive plans with Mia and Ezra. I had specific things I would do with each of them, tiny recalibrations to better suit our particular dynamic. With Mia I'd watch films at the cinema, share popcorn and a drink, take a walk, get dinner in the crew mess after. Mia had energy and she emanated energy. It was something to do with the angles of her face. Ezra was more soporific. We would sit by the staff pool but never swim, or watch television for hours on his bunk. Sometimes we would just hang over the railings and look out at the sea. But if the three of us were all free at the same time, which we rarely were, we'd play Families.

The day I got the memo, I walked home via the boardwalk, the central promenade at the heart of the ship. A sunken stretch flanked by endless tiers of upper decks, filled with lavishly dressed passengers, canopied food vendors and street performers. Large speakers played artificial circus music, blocking out the sound of the sea. It took a long time to move through the crowds. I had arranged to meet Mia and Ezra below deck.

Ezra had a solo cabin, like me. He had covered its already white walls with sheets of white cotton, which hung low and loose. He said he'd done it for the texture. That everything on the ship is so slippery and smooth he feels like a cat in a bath, scrabbling around with nothing to grip on to.

I've left watermelon on the side, he called from the bathroom, when I let myself in. He was on rotation in the staff kitchens and always brought back the leftover fruit.

Mia's running late. He stepped out of the bathroom, pressing a towel to his face. *Do you want to watch TV?*

Ezra was Mia's younger brother, but they were nothing alike. Like Mia, he was olive-skinned, though a lot paler than his sister, as if he had faded. He had the look of a person who is always between things. Sweet-tempered but vague. Sometimes it felt like he was running into you accidentally even when you had arranged to meet. Often, we would be in the middle of a conversation and he would look wide-eyed, suddenly alarmed to find me there at all.

He switched on the T V. Behind him his bed was unmade. Scattered across it was a book about communicating better at work, a teaspoon with a ring-shaped stain, and a polystyrene box containing semi-set smears of ketchup and mustard. Three remaining chips. I noticed he had not yet put on a shirt.

How about Friends? he said. *Or* The Fresh Prince of Bel-Air?

I don't mind, I replied. *Whatever you want is fine.*

I wondered why I always sounded aggressive even when I was trying to be gentle and amenable.

He swept his arm across the duvet and the mess spilled on to the floor. He lay down and shuffled over, his back pressed against the sheet-covered wall. His cabin did not have a window. I lay down beside him and we both stared at the T V. Chandler was stuck in an ATM vestibule with a model. We laughed when he said gum would be perfection. I was tired, close to falling asleep, when without warning Ezra coughed loudly into my hair. I held my hand to the back of my head. I could never tell whether I really loved Ezra or felt sorry for him. I'd always had a hard time distinguishing between pity and love.

I've been chosen, I said.

Chosen for what?

For the thing, I said. *As if you have to ask.*

Oh right. I didn't know you'd applied.

I did, yeah.

Oh well, he sighed. *Good.*

A cat jumped on Ross's back. Ross tried to shrug it off but it clung on anyway. He was wearing a sunset-coloured sweatshirt.

What time will Mia be getting here? I asked.

Soon.

Despite being the person in the world I was most comfortable with, Mia still made me extremely nervous. For a long while I thought this was because she was very beautiful but more recently I realized it was because she doesn't care whether or not she is liked. Ezra once said to me, *It's nice to be nice.* And I agree, it is nice to be nice. I get a lot out of the camaraderie of mutual niceness. It means people don't look at you for too long. But to Mia it simply holds no appeal. Sometimes you can almost see her making the decision to be unkind.

You know what I wish, Ezra said, raising his voice over Monica, who was hysterical about biscuit crumbs or ink stains or something. *I wish all of these sheets would fall on me. And I would be so perfectly swaddled.*

We could do that if you wanted.

He coughed against my neck again.

I heard the sound of Mia outside the door. Heard her exhale, push her keycard into the lock.

Mia! I shouted, as she came in.

Hello, she said, making the word sound heavy and long, before falling horizontally across us.

I met Mia at induction. We were put in pairs and told to make eye contact for a full five minutes. It was supposed to generate employee intimacy and trust. I thought about my husband. How I'd scroll through his search history instead of asking why he was in a bad mood. How I'd masturbate quickly, quietly, in the bathroom, instead of asking him for sex. I did not want to make eye contact with Mia. I did not want to make eye contact with anyone.

I'd previously imagined eye contact as a kind of mutual forward momentum, meeting in the middle. Two stone cherubs spitting at each other, on either side of an ornamental fountain. Their torrents uniting in the centre. But as I stared into Mia's eyes I understood it is not something that exists in an equilibrium. It is more like one person spitting into another person's mouth. An advancer and a receiver.

And I had as much choice in receiving her gaze as a sick pet has gagging back antibiotics syringed into the side of its mouth. I recalled a boy at school, crossing the concrete yard, announcing, *You are my girlfriend now.* How I was his girlfriend for two years. I guess I respected it. You, I needed to be told. You are the one for me. I'd felt like that was what Mia was saying.

Have you heard her news? Ezra said.

Mia twisted around, lying on her back.

What news? she said. *What's your news? If you have news you should tell me.*

I've been chosen.

Chosen? she said. *Oh, wait. Chosen?*

I nodded. Ezra leaned over. *Do you want some watermelon, Mia? There's watermelon on the side.*

I'm OK, Ezra, she said. *So how do you feel about it? Did you find out today? So the ceremony will be tomorrow?*

I guess, I said. *And yeah, I feel good about it. I dunno. We don't need to talk about it.*

Wow, Mia said, sitting up, then standing. *Why you?*

What do you mean?

I just mean why did they choose you?

That's what I thought you meant, I said.

Not like that. I mean, I thought they only chose people who are sort of . . . exceptional?

Can we start Families now, Ezra interrupted. *I'm getting tired.*

Mia turned to stare at him. *Sure,* she said, drily.

Families works like this. Someone is the mum. Someone is the dad. Someone is the baby. I don't know how we came up with it, it just sort of happened, and after a while we formalized it with a name. We'd take it in turns being the characters but we all agreed being the baby was best. If we were feeling tired or uninventive we'd just lay whoever was the baby out on the bed and bring them food and give them a bottle of whatever we had to drink and stroke their hair and whisper reassuring things into their ears. If we were feeling more imaginative we would work out a more complicated scenario. Something like, the dad has recently become aware of the mum's ongoing infidelity but has decided not to confront her about it, and the mum has found a lump in her left breast which has triggered a latent eating disorder, and the baby has acid reflux and is not sleeping at all.

We weren't feeling up to much that evening so we went with the standard set-up. It was my turn to be the baby. Ezra was the mum and Mia was the dad. Mia arranged me on the bed and held the back of her hand to my forehead.

Mum, she said. *I think she's got a temperature.*

Oh really? Ezra replied. *Because she's been fine with me all day.*

He sat at the base of my feet and felt along my calves.

I suppose she's a little clammy, he said. *Could you get me a cold compress?*

Mia went into the tiny bathroom and emerged with a piece of muslin cloth, soaked and wrung out with water. She handed it to Ezra, who stood up and blotted my face.

There there, he said. *I didn't realize you were feeling poorly, little one.* He tenderly placed the damp cloth across my forehead. *I hope she's not caught anything. There are some nasty things going around.*

I'm sure she's fine, Mia replied. *We'll keep an eye on her.*

Can you please keep your voice down? Ezra said. *You always do this. Storm in and shout.*

I'm not shouting, Mia said, in a loud whisper. *Is this better?*

Much better, Ezra said. *Thank you.*

I lay back, enjoying the cool weight of the compress. The ship was gently rocking. I began drifting off. I tuned in and out of a conversation Mia and Ezra were having about how Mia was always taking me out of the house with wet hair.

I was woken by Ezra running a fingertip along my upper arm. *Time for something to eat*, he said, holding out a bottle of aloe vera water. Mia placed a hand under my head, which I tilted back, as Ezra fed me the bottle. It was only about a quarter full and I drank what was left even though it was unpleasantly viscous and sweet. After I had finished, Mia dabbed at my mouth with a towel.

Good girl, she said.

Good girl, Ezra echoed. He propped me up, rubbed my back in circles. I released a small burp in response. *That's it*, he said. *Let it all out.*

Shall we try you on some watermelon? Mia said, holding a triangle of pink, wet fruit. I covered my teeth with my lips and bit at it. The juice ran down my chin and neck. Mia used the towel to clean me.

You silly thing, she said.

You missed a spot, Ezra said. *Here, let me do it.*

He took the towel from Mia and began wiping my mouth more industriously. Then he returned it to Mia.

Can we finish up now? she said, dropping the towel and breaking character. Pulp Fiction*'s on at twelve.*

~~~~~

I had applied to Keith's mentoring programme after a notification informed me I was eligible. When I saw it pop up on my tablet, I looked around the empty room for evidence of some sort of administrative error, before realizing, yes, I was, and always had been, just a little bit better than my colleagues. Just a little more invested. Just a little more enthused. It was why my cabin had a window and theirs did not. There was no question about it, I was going to apply.

There were three parts to it. First, an aptitude test. The standard logic and psychometric exercises you might expect. Rows of squares partially blacked out waiting to be put into order. Pretend news articles about the state of the automobile industry or the French Revolution that you had to make sense of. Second, a video portion in which you had to record yourself saying why you wanted to join the programme. Finally, an essay on what wabi sabi meant to you, and how you adhered to its principles throughout your daily living. The first part was tricky. I thought of myself as more clever than most, but so were the majority of the staff on board. The second part was a little easier. I had done all the available customer-service training. I knew how to sound interested in things. I also knew that the final part, the essay, would be what landed it.

I thought for a long while, moving slowly around my cabin. I considered eating a rotten apple, describing the flavour, the crystalline golden hue. But then I remembered my toothbrush, the bottom of which had snapped off a few months ago. I wrote about how it was somehow more beautiful that way, that its deficits gave it charm, an undeniable kind of grace. I wrote about how I'd broken it by yanking it too quickly out of my mouth, that it had snapped one of my teeth too. How I had studied the scalloped edge of it, a small pearl in my hand. I wrote that it was an accident but look where we are. Once I'd pressed Send I went to the bathroom and threw my toothbrush in the bin. On my tablet, I pulled up the resources tab and ordered a new one.

~~~~~

The morning after I saw Mia and Ezra, I was given permission to miss my shift in order to attend the initiation ceremony. It was held in Keith's office, on the top deck. In the waiting room were a handful of other people who I assumed had also been selected for the programme. His receptionist signed me in, offered me strawberry mochi and cucumber water without looking up from her computer. Her uniform was prim and neat, a blank canvas of efficiency. In front of her desk were several rows of straight-backed chairs, and behind them, a ring of flat cushions strewn on the floor. I took a glass of water and a piece of mochi shaped like a kitten and retreated to a cushion, sitting cross-legged and biting off the mochi's head, its sleeping eyes and inked-on mouth. I sipped the cucumber water. It tasted bitter and old. Fibrous strands of cucumber wrapped themselves around my molars.

I looked around the room. There were ten of us in total. I recognized two of the women waiting, Madeleine and Kai, plus a man with a mole at the absolute centre of his chin. I had worked with Madeleine in the kitchens and shared a rotation with Kai at one of the lower-deck casinos. I remembered little about Madeleine but could vividly recall the casino. High heels sinking into pile carpeting. Gaudy lighting and men weeping on the phone. The smell of Kai's hair, acidic, like cheap wine. I couldn't place the man, though we nodded at each other in mutual acknowledgement. The brief camaraderie triggered a hum deep in my stomach, and I could not determine whether it was anxiety or excitement. I once heard that a good way to cope with anxiety is to just pretend it is excitement. The body's articulation is the same either way. You can trick your brain into practically anything.

The receptionist called Kai's name and she stood up, then raised her shoulders to demonstrate some level of trepidation. Keith's voice could be heard as the door opened and closed. It made me feel anxious. Or perhaps excited.

I got up and helped myself to another piece of mochi, this time shaped like a rabbit. I sat back down and put it into my mouth, realizing too late that I had run out of water, that I could not go up to the desk a third time. I kept chewing and chewing as the mochi failed to change in size or constitution. After a little while I gave up and, when nobody was looking, I spat it into my sleeve where it fastened like a living thing to the underside of my wrist. Everyone was either staring at their tablets or closing their eyes as if to meditate and I felt at once relieved that my humiliation had gone unnoticed and entirely alone in dealing with this nightmare. Eventually, Kai emerged looking flush-faced and teary and my name was called. I stood up, taking great care not to let the mochi slip out from beneath my sleeve. Life is hell, I thought, as I entered the room.

It was quite a small space. Keith was sat behind his desk, which was mostly empty, with the exception of two small bowls and a large iron teapot with an indented bamboo handle, arranged on a serving tray made from a sliced-out ring of tree trunk. I sat down like a very sweet girl. Keith loomed over the table, taller than I remembered. My mind immediately went towards thoughts on whether or not I found him attractive, and if I did not, whether that would be enough to dissuade me from having sex with him, should the opportunity ever arise. I hoped nothing could be read from my face. I braided my fingers in my lap.

Ingrid, Keith said. *Please take a seat.*

Thank you, I replied. *But I am already sitting.*

I see, he said. *Well please make yourself comfortable.*

I rounded my shoulders and arched my back until I felt as close to comfortable as I could imagine. I waited for him to say more.

I am grateful for this opportunity, I offered, attempting a smile. The mochi pressed moistly against my wrist.

Grateful, Keith said. *Grateful is an interesting choice of word.*

He stood up and lifted the teapot. He made a show of swirling its contents around. He reminded me of my dad post-retirement, clumsily materteral, fussing around the back of the sofa. I gazed up at him as he poured tea into the bowls. It smelled like soy sauce and herbs. He took his seat once again, and gestured for me to take a bowl. I reached forward to hold it with both hands, instinctively blowing on the translucent brown liquid. He took the other bowl, cupping it against his chest, self-consciously cute, the way large men are when they do something girlish.

You know the etymology of the word grateful, Keith said, *comes from the Saxon word grot. And that means large. To be filled up with a feeling of largeness. Isn't that interesting?*

It is, I said. *It is interesting.*

He leaned forward to sniff the tea. The *WA* was swaying ever so slightly, the room moving back and forth. He lifted the bowl to his lips and took a sip, closing his eyes to savour the taste. He knew I was watching. He opened his eyes slowly, like someone coming round from a deep meditation.

Something that I like to think about, he said, *is the singularity of a moment. Do you ever think about that?*

I don't, I said, apologetic.

Well perhaps you should.

He placed the bowl back on the table and looked at it. It was moss-green, slightly asymmetric. It gleamed when it caught the light.

This bowl is called a chawan.

I nodded.

That's Japanese, he said.

Ah, I replied.

That's Japanese for bowl.

He ran his finger around the lip of the bowl, its dips and peaks, like a slowly rotating landscape. Then he tilted it back to show me the matte underside.

Ingrid, he said. *Are you aware of the Japanese aesthetic tradition of wabi sabi?*

Yes, I replied quickly. *I am.*

Indulge me, he said.

I sat up straight. I was attentive and willing to please, and there seemed to me no reason to pretend otherwise.

Everything is going into and coming out of nothingness, I recited.

That's right, he said. He rubbed his face then brought the bowl back to his lips. *You know I've been to Japan.* He paused and looked thoughtfully off to one side. *A few times, actually.*

Wow, I said.

How about you? he asked. *Have you ever been to Japan?*

No.

You really should go, he said. *If you get the chance.*

I will, I said.

He nodded. *Drink your tea.*

My eyes fell to my own chawan. It was rain-grey and uneven. It didn't gleam when it caught the light. I lifted it to my mouth and sipped some of the tea. Fragrant and light on the tongue, with a strange aftertaste. I took comfort in the heaviness of the bowl, like how I'd get my husband to lie on top of me when I was having a panic attack. Keith levelled his gaze at me from across the table, a horizon coming into view.

It's strange to think, he said, *the same accident of design that led to the creation of this bowl is no different to the accident of you and I being alive.*

I blinked into the bowl, noticed dark sediment pooling at the bottom. I moved it from side to side, disrupting the soft grit, previously still and contained.

That's something to think about, Keith said. *Isn't it?*

I smiled at him expansively. *It really is*, I said.

A few moments passed and I watched Keith make up his mind about me. He reached over to remove my empty bowl and stacked it within his own, putting them both to one side. Then he smiled back at me, smiling like I was a person who was elusive and vague but who ultimately got it.

There's something about you, he said. *Though I'm not sure what.*

Thank you, I said.

You're welcome. A lot of people wouldn't have taken that as a compliment.

I'll take what I can get, I replied.

Keith seemed momentarily embarrassed. For the first time it occurred to me that I might be older than him, and I wondered whether that meant I had some sort of duty of care.

So this is the programme, he said. *And you're in. Congratulations.*

Thank you.

You've already said that. He frowned. *And you're still welcome.*

He extended his hand to me and I shook it. The wet mochi bulged beneath my sleeve. I'd forgotten all about it and was strangely relieved to find it still there, clinging to my wrist like it wasn't afraid to stay with me. I turned to show myself out, pushing open the door.

Ingrid, Keith called from behind the desk. *Don't forget to be the best you you can be. OK?*

I turned back towards him and nodded seriously.

I won't, I said.

I was grateful. I really was.

~~~~~

When I went back to work later that afternoon the gift shop smelled of salt and was rocking forcefully. We were coming out of a period of relatively calm weather but now things seemed always to move. This made me nervous on account of the fact I was not a strong swimmer. Or perhaps more accurately, I had never actually learned to swim. There was only one question about it as part of the application process, and obviously I lied, said I'd spent summers splashing around in hotel pools, went to the seaside every bank holiday. It was not, to my mind, a big deal.

We had protocols for when the ship was pitching or rolling heavily, but much of it was up to our own common sense. At which point did we consider the choppiness to be a liability, and when were we prepared to address it. By the time I arrived, Zach was already running around gathering small objects into wire shopping baskets. *Trinkets!* he shouted when he saw me. *For Christ sake, Ingrid, help me protect the trinkets!* I watched him ineffectually pluck tiny clocks embedded into semi-precious stones and old cans of tuna refurbished into pillboxes from the shelves. He had been on this rotation longer than I had and I found his ineptitude repulsive.

I kept half an eye on him but didn't move from behind the register, scrolling through old messages with Mia on my tablet. The shop kept rocking. Zach continued putting things away.

The glassware, I instructed, coming to. *It's the glassware that needs doing first.*

Oh god, he said. *I'm so sorry. I didn't think.*

It's fine, I said, but I hoped he knew it was not. *You do the champagne flutes and I'll do everything else.*

OK, he said.

And please remember to handle them by the stem, I said. *I don't want a fiasco like last time.*

Of course not, he replied. *I'll handle them by the stem, I'll handle them by the stem.*

I stepped out from behind the counter and cautiously approached the rattling glassware. I picked up one of the champagne flutes, holding the stem between my index and thumb.

Like this, I said.

Zach half-ran towards me. He picked one up.

Like this? he said.

His hand was shaking.

Very good, I said. *Exactly like that. But please don't run.*

I smiled in a way I found excruciating and began tidying away the whisky tumblers and highball glasses. We had foam-lined crates to store them in when the ship got rocky. I plucked them from the shelves, slid them into the soft, squeaking gaps. It was work I was good at. I'd attended a workshop called Fluid Movement, which was all about relaxing into the waves and not working against them. It was based on bon odori, a type of Japanese traditional dance. It could increase productivity during storms by thirty per cent. Mia told me about it. She told me it was optional but that considering I would be working in the gift shop it was in my best interests to attend. We were told the ocean was not something we should fight but something we should lean into. We were shown how to do that, how to move with the waves. At the end of the session we were asked to lie on the floor, and feel the sea support us. *The sea will always support you*, the lady said. *It is as solid as the ground beneath your feet.*

Behind me I heard a crash, just a small one. I turned around to see Zach, devastated, surrounded by smashed glass. Blue and green in the light, like the body of a fly. I walked calmly over and helped him collect the larger fragments and put them into the bin. I liked putting things in bins. There! I would think. In the bin! Where bad things go! I liked bins very much, generally.

We could go quicker if you weren't shaking so much, I told him.

Everything took so long. Everything seemed to take an eternity but we had so little time. Why was he still shaking?

You are shaking too, he said. *You know you are shaking too, right?*

I looked at the glass in my hand, vibrating, and realized, I am shaking. I am shaking too.

~~~~

I had the evening free and so did Mia. We arranged to eat dinner in the crew mess. I was tired after a sore and slow-moving day. I'd found myself periodically lingering near the miniature bottles of spirits, but I did not let myself think about how much easier the day would be if I was drunk.

We'd arranged to meet in the queue, whoever arrived first claiming a spot. But when I entered the canteen and saw the huge, undulating chain of people I semi-recognized, I had the feeling of standing on the edge of fast-moving rapids, too scared to jump in.

Mia came up behind me and stepped into the line. Everything about Mia was very small, her neat little head and haircut, her short, sallow limbs. She slipped easily into narrow spaces, no need to ask anyone to make room. I thought it gave her a warped perspective on the world. I manoeuvred myself in behind her. The woman behind me shuffled begrudgingly back and I was able to stand up straight. I waited for my breathing to steady. Mia turned to acknowledge me.

Everything all right? she asked wearily, as though everything was obviously not all right, and it was frustrating this was so often the case.

Yeah fine, I said. *Bit tired because I got up early.*

What did you do that for? she replied.

I went for a run.

Good for you, she said. Then, after a little while, rolled her eyes.

We neared the buffet. Quarters of cabbage were lined up like soft and translucent tortoises. Neat sleeves of ham, pink and curled. A tray of silver fish, white eyes fixed on nothing, jewelled with sea salt and herbs. I briefly wondered what five years of days-old food was doing to my insides.

I'm going to have the fish, I said. *Ezra told me it was good.*

Of course he did, Mia replied. *Ezra loves salt.*

He does. He is probably going to die soon.

Mia turned to face me, holding a pair of silver tongs. *Don't say that*, she said. *What would you say that for?*

The queue moved us along as I tried not to feel childish and embarrassed. We peered over the large trays of food to see what else was on offer. Smoked feta and almonds. Fennel with pear and dill. Quinoa and bee pollen. Yorkshire puddings and bone broth. The recipes always sounded delicious but everything just tasted of monosodium glutamate, either singed or unpleasantly wilted, from hours beneath the hot buffet lamps.

You should have the broth, Mia said. *Make sure you have a bowl of the broth.*

I looked at her hesitantly. *Amino acids*, she said, flatly.

When we reached the front of the queue I collected a small white bowl and obediently filled it with broth. I went to get one for Mia but she quickly placed her hand on my wrist and shook her head.

You should be regularly eating bone. But I don't really need to.

I continued filling my tray. I took some of the feta, a little cabbage, a single Yorkshire pudding. Mia filled her entire plate with creamed spinach.

It's what I fancied, she said, shrugging.

We took a seat in the back corner, our usual spot, sat across from each other. I started drinking my soup. In the background I could hear some music, either the Police or Prince. I couldn't remember the last time I had listened to music I myself had chosen. I wondered what I might choose if given the chance. Perhaps it would be the Police. Or Prince.

This running? she said. *Is it part of the programme? It doesn't sound like it's part of the programme.*

It's not, I replied. *But it sort of is. I'm trying to get ready.*

I tore into my Yorkshire pudding. It felt more like fabric than food. Like something you could sleep in.

I feel like I would be ready, she said. *Like if I was on the programme, I would already be ready.*

Did you apply? I asked.

I'm not ambitious, she retorted. *People are always saying I'm ambitious but it's not really the case.*

This was something Mia liked to say about herself. She once told me people were always mistaking her desire to be the very best at whatever job she was doing for ambition. She told me most people fundamentally didn't understand ambition and what it meant, but she did, and it was not for her. I watched her across the table, straight-backed, eating spinach in measured spoonfuls. She looked fresh-faced and healthy. A stock photo of a woman answering the phone. I wondered, if this was not ambition then what was?

So you didn't apply, then?

Of course I applied. She set down her spoon. *I always apply.*

I looked around the crew mess. On one side was the canteen with the service counter and the metal vats of food. At the end of that was a little drinks service. There were other things too, a gong and a large beanbag beneath it. A boxed Japanese rock garden and smooth wooden rake. There was a basketball hoop and several balls. There was a broken loom.

People are always getting me wrong, Mia repeated.

She stood up and walked across the room, returning with a glass of wine and a plastic cup of squash. She placed the squash in front of me. Iridescent and perfumed.

People say I am extroverted because I'm very confident and I like atten-tion and praise. But actually, I am quite introverted.

I watched Mia sip her wine, imagined the flush feeling of being reset. I held the squash to my mouth, coating my lips in chemicals and sugar.

So what happened? she said. *The ceremony? It was this morning?*

It was weird. I had some mochi then he told me I should be the best me I could be.

And?

And then we drank tea which tasted like soy sauce.

Mia rolled her eyes for the fourth or perhaps fifth time that even-ing. *I'm sure that's just your unrefined Western palate*, she said. She moved spinach around her plate, gulped more wine. *You know that's good advice. You should be keeping a note of all of the advice he gives you.*

I am, I said.

Sometimes I worry about how seriously you take your future, she replied. *You and Ezra. You're like a pair of walking clouds. It probably would have been better for all of us if I was the one doing this.*

Perhaps.

You're extremely lucky, she continued. *This thing with Keith. You've been given this amazing opportunity and it's basically just fallen into your lap.*

Well, not exactly.

More or less, Mia said.

She scraped the lip of her spoon around the circumference of her plate, consolidating the remaining specks of spinach. *Do you want to play some basketball?*

We took our trays to the refuse area, scraped them down, then rinsed them off with water. We topped our glasses up and made towards the basketball hoop. Standing beneath it, Mia grabbed my wrist.

I love you, she announced. *You know I love you, right?*

I love you too, Mia, I replied. *Of course I do.*

Well, good, she said. *I've just been thinking, it's really important we start saying it more. We should say it every time we see each other. We should say* I love you. *Now you go.*

OK, I said. *I love you.*

Good, she said, unblinking. *Well done.*

I retrieved a basketball from the stand and threw it towards the hoop but it didn't even hit the rim. It rolled towards us and Mia picked it up, focused her gaze on the hoop and threw. The ball fell neatly through the centre of the ring without touching the sides. She didn't look surprised or victorious. She looked like a person confirming information they already knew.

~~~~~

Ezra's cabin was bigger than mine though it felt much smaller because of the lack of a window. Mia had the largest cabin of us all, though she shared with three room-mates, all women, none of whom she had anything nice to say about. Still, she elected to stay with them even though she had been given the option of a solo cabin many, many times.

I had the smallest but I didn't mind. It had a window, a tiny port-hole, a round and unending vista of the ocean, so it always felt expansive and cool. There was something animal and safe-feeling about it. It was very different from how I used to feel in my flat, the one I shared with my husband. It was a flat that felt more like a house, spread out as it was across three levels. High ceilings and floorboards. Pantry behind the kitchen. My cabin contained just two rooms and felt more natural for it. My bedroom had a single bed, underneath it a sliding cupboard, then a slim white wardrobe, small desk, mushroom-shaped desk lamp. My bathroom had a chemical toilet with a showerhead situated directly over it. A drain slightly to the side and then a basin. If I stood at the right spot I could touch every wall of my cabin without moving my feet, including the ceiling and floor.

It only occasionally felt claustrophobic and in those moments I had been known to attempt to open the porthole, once with a felt-tip pen and a caulking mallet, another time with a snail fork lifted from a shift. I'd get Ezra to help me. I'd wedge the tip of the felt-tip pen or the prongs of the fork into the gap between the window and the wall while Ezra smacked down on it with the mallet. The felt-tip pen splintered apart in my hand, the snail fork bent to one side and the caulking mallet left a dent in the metal frame, but of course it didn't open. Though I liked to think it might have.

I'd been in this cabin for three years and on the *WA* for five. Each year we were given the option of taking our leave on shore or remaining on ship. If we elected to holiday on shore we would lose our allocated cabin, but if we took our leave on ship we were guaranteed to keep it for another year. I didn't want to risk losing my cabin. Also I had nowhere else to go.

When I planned to spend any stretch of time in my cabin, which is mostly what I planned, I was comforted by imagining the scope of my options as the image-cropping tool on my tablet, narrowing in on a single subject. My options were, realistically, watch or read something, stare out of the porthole, or have a nap. It made me feel like a child picking a toy from a very small toy box. Even if I started doing something else, eventually I'd wind up staring out of the porthole.

I was both entirely sick and not at all sick of looking at the sea. It remained familiar and surprising at the same time, something bodily, like illness or a sneeze. I found it soothingly obliterating, like listening to white noise on the Tube home from work. I particularly liked watching when the sea was rough and the waves slapped against the glass like carbonated tentacles. I never minded it being rocky. I liked the feeling of being violently urged to sleep. Feeling my body move from side to side like a metronome. I'd lose track of the time, come to realizing I was an hour further advanced into being alive. It was like crossing a chore from a list. Done!

Another thing that was consistently pleasing about watching the sea from my cabin was the crisp feeling of being completely and irrefutably dry. I liked to hold my hand up to my face to confirm its aridity. I had to maintain my cabin at quite a low temperature to ensure I did not perspire. I would have kept showers to a minimum too, if a daily shower were not mandatory, but all kinds of grooming and cleansing were mandatory on the *WA*. I had to brush my hair, pluck my eyebrows. I had to wear sparse, elegant make-up. I suppose none of these things were unusual.

What was unusual was that I didn't have any of my own clothes. On rotations I was issued a uniform according to whatever job I was doing. When I wasn't working I wore the *WA* leisure-time tracksuit, a soft hooded top and elasticated trousers. To sleep I wore powder-blue cropped bottoms and button-down shirts. Only on land did I feel compelled to dress myself, usually just buying something from the first shop I saw, then throwing it away when I was done. I quite enjoyed not being burdened by possessions, my identity unmoored from an assembly of material.

Before the *WA* my sense of self was so tentative that a pair of jeans I'd forgotten to belt or a shirt I didn't like my arms in could make me feel scattered and anxious. Not one person but several, warring it out underneath my skin. I wasted hours matching skirts to blouses, finding long-sleeved T-shirts to wear beneath pinafores. I had a whole drawer just for earrings, a wardrobe just for coats. On the *WA* it felt good to slip on my communications suit or my catering tunic or my healthcare assistant scrubs and lean into the texture of my day. Sometimes I'd watch the passengers of the ship and the sheer variety of colour in their clothes made me feel like my eyes were too slowly adjusting from darkness to light. Retiring my wardrobe had been one of the great liberations of the *WA*, of which there were many.

Before the start of a shift I'd set my alarm an hour earlier than I needed to. A friend once told me the reason you struggle to get out of bed in the morning is because all the particles of dust from the air have come to rest on top of your body while you sleep. When you wake up you are blanketed by a thick, invisible weight. I thought about that a lot as I lay in bed in the mornings, trying to force myself to sit up. I imagined the particles as a heavy duvet of dead skin and salt air, and it felt good to know there was a reason it was so hard.

Once up I'd make myself a cup of coffee, which I could do without having to leave my bed. I could do a lot of stuff without having to leave my bed. I'd reach over to switch on my small kettle, stir instant coffee into long-life milk. If it was daytime I would sit back and drink it looking out at the sea. If it was night-time I would watch my own reflection. Scythes of colour and light smudged across the blackened window. Thin droplets of seawater clinging to the other side. I liked the pink-faced feeling of having just woken up, dreams spilling into waking life, a day moon bobbing in the sky. I'd spend only a little time getting ready and I'd shower only because I had to. I brushed and dried my hair and if I had a little time left over I lay back down on my bed and tried very hard not to lurch back into sleep. I set a second alarm for when I had to leave my cabin.

Each rotation lasted an indeterminate length of time, sometimes a few weeks, sometimes a couple of years. We were eligible for all jobs on ship, with the exception of work that required *heavy specialization*. Chief engineer or on-board surgeon or head chef were not part of the rotations. Before I was a customer service assistant, I was an IT administrator. Before that I was an environmental officer. Before that I was a croupier. Before that I was an able seaman. Before that I was a cocktail waitress. Before that I was a librarian. Before that I was a portrait photographer. I wasn't good at any of these jobs, none of us were, but that wasn't the point. We were good at pretending.

I had one week left before I rotated over to become a manicurist. We were expected to prepare for our next rotation during the current one. We usually did this while on duty. In the gift shop, I often propped my tablet on top of the cash register during slow periods, one eye on a tutorial, the other on the shop floor. Otherwise I sloped off and pretended to tidy the changing rooms and just sat in there.

Each job had its own guidebook, accessible via our tablets, which we were required to take everywhere, and each guidebook contained a selection of one-pagers and diagrams and frequently asked questions and short video tutorials to get us ready. Within the guide there were core modules and there were optional ones. We had the opportunity, here, to make our jobs our own. And it was always worth doing a few optional modules. They were the fun ones.

The fresh-flower training was one of them. It was a two-hour module. It included content on the temperature and quality of the water in the vase, how to arrange the flowers, and how to maintain them over a longer period of time. Flowers thrive in clean, warm water. Warm water dissolves air bubbles which may have formed in the stems and allows for more efficient absorption. It also allows any added flower food to dissolve more quickly. The stems should be cut one inch from the bottom, at a relatively sharp angle, to increase the surface area through which the flower can take in water.

Before arranging the flowers you have to order them by quantity. If you have more hydrangeas than any other flower then you will be placing those in the vase first. Then you add the next most abundant type of flower, and so on. Criss-crossing the stems will create a sense of volume in the middle of the bouquet. To maintain your bouquet you can add sugar water, vinegar or more warm water. You can also remove any petals that look dead or dying. You should periodically mist them.

The training contained a combination of light botany and interior decor. On completion, I was qualified to arrange flowers on any deck of the ship. I was not, however, qualified to arrange occasion or event flowers. But I told myself I would cross that bridge when I came to it.

~~~~~

Not long after my induction into the programme, I received notice of another appointment with Keith. It was to be held in his office like the last time. It was requested that I wear non-uniform clothing so Keith would have a better idea of the *raw material he was dealing with*. I borrowed a fitted black dress and a pair of kitten heels from Mia, momentarily wondering why she had them, suspecting it was not the right moment to ask.

The morning of the meeting I sat down to look at my face in the mirror, cataloguing the problems that needed solving. Often, looking at my face gave me a strong sense of rage, not necessarily directed at my face itself, but an abstract, unfocused rage, where my face just happened to be the thing it was pointing towards. But I didn't feel anger as I readied myself for the programme, rather I felt a calm kind of curiosity. I tried seeing myself through Keith's eyes to make a judgement as he might. I was wearing simple make-up, thin channels of eyeliner and a pale lipstick. I looked around my cabin, trying to see other things through his eyes, the face creams lined up in order of use, the pile of unwashed underwear in the corner. I wondered whether Keith might look at himself in a mirror trying to see through my eyes. Whether anyone would.

I arrived at his office a little early, again, and was once more seated in the waiting room. There was another decanter of water, this time with mint leaves wilted at the bottom. The mochi was chocolate and shaped like little mice. I took the glass of water but declined the mochi. I sipped carefully so that I would have some left when Keith called me in. He would see me with the glass still half-full, witness my restraint, and think fondly of me as the kind of person that doesn't just devour a thing wherever they find it. I looked around the room, faces familiar from the last meeting. Madeleine and Kai both working hard not to look at me or each other. The man with the mole, biting his nails. I pictured the other waiting rooms I had sat in, instinctively suspicious of the people sitting around me. I had heard not everyone sees the programme all the way through. Some people are less inclined to hand large parts of themselves over, to something, to anything, I suppose.

I became suddenly conscious of my empty glass and, worse, a strand of mint leaf stuck between my teeth. I had not been paying attention and now there was no way of sluicing mint from my mouth without a drink. I imagined Keith opening his office door to invite me in, finding me maniacally helping myself to a second glass of water. And I couldn't risk mining my teeth with my fingernails, hunched over like a feeding animal. Instead, I acquiesced to the reality of the mint leaf remaining in situ, a pin loosened from a hand grenade but held more or less in place. I did not feel relaxed any more.

In the end Keith did not come out of his office to fetch me, instead, his receptionist informed me I should go inside. Idiot, I thought. I should have remembered this from the last time.

Keith was sitting at his desk as I walked in. His eyes were fixed to the screen of his laptop. His hands scrambled across the keys. He didn't look up at me and yet indicated via some small flex of his face that he wanted me to sit down. Everything he did seemed subtly skilled, learned at business school or passed down by a mentor of his own. It did not surprise me that he was monumentally successful.

I positioned my hands in my lap, imagining myself a child in a Pre-Raphaelite painting, a small, pale dog at my side. I wanted him to see me for what I was, or at least, what I could be. Measured. Pliant. In possession of potential. I slowed my breathing and rehearsed some anodyne remarks, observations on the weather etc., interrupted as he hit one of the keys hard, with an air of pointed finality. I wondered which character he'd pressed. Probably an exclamation mark. I wondered whether I should start signing off messages with an exclamation mark. It seemed assertive. He looked up from his desk.

Take a seat, he said.

I have, I said.

I hoped he didn't think I was being condescending and so I pointedly repositioned myself into the absolute centre of the chair. I pulled my dress further down my legs, regretting borrowing my outfit from Mia, who liked to wear clothes a little tighter than I did, something I tried not to hold against her. I folded one leg over the other, hoping the dress would not rip. Keith was watching me, palms against the polished wood of his desk, blinking intently. I wondered what he wanted from me, what he wanted from any of us. I wondered how I could demonstrate I was willing to accommodate that desire, that I was willing to accommodate most desires. I looked down at my legs, bundled in black fabric. I knew I presented as a fundamentally gullible person.

So let me tell you how this works, Keith said. *You're going to tell me something. Something about your life. Something that happened to you. And I am going to listen.*

I gazed across the table. *What sort of thing do I tell you?*

You can tell me anything you like, he said. *But usually there will be a theme or I will ask you a question.*

I can do that, I replied.

Let's begin with a memory. Can you tell me about something you remember? Maybe even the last thing you remember before joining the WA*?*

I creased my forehead, trying to picture my life before the *WA*. I could remember vague feelings, loose physical sensations, but I couldn't think of anything that had actually happened.

Or something before that, Keith added. *Anything from before you came here.*

I closed my eyes and focused. My mind felt like a piece of paper with a line drawn vertically down the middle. I was trying to populate the first column but the second column kept writing itself. Things I didn't want to remember. Things I had tried very hard to forget. I focused harder on the first column. Eventually I remembered something, a relatively small incident, something that had happened in the flat. It returned to me with unsettling clarity, the contours of my husband's face, the colour of the walls. There was something about the colour of those rooms that would give me a bone-deep nausea whenever I thought about them, the dark sea-green. It made me think of violins tuning or the quiet after a long cry. The colour of exhaustion and melancholy. The more I thought about it the more I felt my guts move, spasms of dissent. Still, my mind couldn't stop sketching in the blanks, the clock that we'd found in a flea market, the record player with the lid left open. A horde of pixels filling in the gaps. I didn't know how to make them stop. I opened my eyes.

I've got one, I said.

Wonderful, Keith beamed. *Tell me about it.*

OK. I had been arguing with my husband. We were sitting on the sofa, watching television. My husband was flipping through a book and I was looking at my phone. I was messaging my friend while reading something on the internet, an article or something. I was telling my friend that my husband and I were having a hard time, flicking between the messaging app and the browser. And I accidentally sent a message about my husband to him. The message said, He's so fucking annoying. He's being an absolute prick. *As soon as I pressed Send I heard my husband's phone vibrate and I knew what I'd done. He didn't react. He just showed me the screen. Then he went to the bathroom.*

Keith closed his eyes as if carefully metabolizing what I had told him. After a while he opened them and looked back over at me. *Again*, he said.

I hesitated. Had I done something wrong? *I'm sorry, Keith . . . I'm not sure I understand?*

He smiled, patient and indulgent. *Sometimes in these sessions I will ask you to repeat yourself. To tell the story again.* He held his hands together and paused. *It's about opening you up. It's a technique I have personally developed. Sometimes we may even tell the story together. Sometimes I will ask you to close your eyes. Sometimes I will want you to look right at me. Sometimes I will invite you to speak while moving around. Sometimes I myself will move around you. Sometimes, Ingrid, we may move around one another.* He made a gesture indicating that this list continued indefinitely.

So, now, he said, *you tell me again about your husband and the message. You should start from the beginning. And this time, try to add in more detail. Try to remember more.*

I closed my eyes as I had done before. I pictured the scene.

I had been arguing with my husband, I said. *We had been arguing for months. We were sitting on the sofa in our living room. Our entire living room was coloured green. Even the curtains were green. Even the sofa was green. My husband was reading a book. I was looking at my phone. I was messaging my friend Ethan while reading something on the internet. I think it was an article about global warming. I was messaging my friend telling him that my husband and I were having a hard time and flicking between the messaging app and the browser. The flicking back and forth was giving me a headache but at that point I had a headache all the time so it didn't really matter. Ethan asked how things were at home. I thought about how to reply to him, half-reading the article on global warming, and when I'd decided what I wanted to write I must have gone into the thread with my husband by accident. And so I sent the message to my husband. The message said,* He's so fucking annoying. He's driving me insane. *As soon as I pressed Send I heard my husband's phone vibrate and I knew what I'd done. His face didn't change but he showed me the screen. Then he stood up and went to the bathroom and closed the door behind him.*

Again, Keith said. His eyes remained open. *And more. Even more.*

I wondered whether I found the exercise tedious or painful, realizing I actually found it cathartic. It felt like chanting, repeating a word until it was emptied of meaning. I began again.

I had been arguing with my husband, I said. *And we had been arguing for months. I don't know how it happened. We had become unbearable to each other. We were sitting on our sofa, in our green fucking living room. Everything was green. My husband was reading a book about being a more effective manager. I was messaging my friend Ethan, who I was also fucking. At the same time I was reading something about global warming on the internet. It was about grain. It was about how land temperature was making it harder for farmers to grow certain types of grain. That in China certain types of grain production, rice, wheat and corn, were now near impossible.*

I kept flicking between the messaging app and the browser. The flicking back and forth was giving me a headache but then I always had a headache so I didn't really notice. Ethan had sent me a message asking how things were at home. I thought about how to reply to him, and I needed to think about it because he was the only person I could speak to honestly, and yet I knew speaking badly about your husband to your friend who you are also fucking is not exactly classy. And also because I wanted him to keep liking me. I wanted him to keep wanting to fuck me.

I stared at this article about global warming but I was thinking about how to reply. When I'd decided what I wanted to write I opened up the messaging app, but instead of choosing the conversation between me and Ethan I went into the thread with my husband. I typed out my reply to Ethan's question and that reply said, I hate him. *I knew I was sending the message to my husband as I pressed Send. I know that I knew before I heard his phone vibrate. Somewhere in my brain I had registered the previous message in the conversation and it had said,* Chicken or lamb? *He didn't react. He just showed me the screen. And then he went to the bathroom for an hour.*

Keith had closed his eyes again while I spoke and I was glad of it. Not because I didn't want a witness but because I also liked to close my eyes in company sometimes. To shut everything out. To give my brain a rest. He nodded, opened his eyes.

Thank you, he said. *That cannot have been easy.*

I turned to look out the window. The sky was clear and the sea was still. Just two strips of blue, one paler than the other. Contained in a rectangle like a nation's flag.

It's a beautiful view, isn't it? Keith said.

I nodded.

I've had a thought, he said. *There's one more thing to do.*

He got up and went over to the sideboard, rummaged around and came back with a paperweight. It was an object I recognized from my induction, years ago.

A symbolic gesture, he said, handing it to me. *To get us started on this journey.*

Of course, I said, accepting the gift. It was a metallic sphere, plain and unremarkable. I could keep it on my desk.

Well. Where is your tablet? Show it to me, please.

I reached down to my side, where the slim lozenge of metal and glass rested against my chair leg.

What did we do before all this? he said, smiling benignly. *I bet you have your whole life in this device. Technology has made our lives so much easier. There are algorithms that can predict the weather. That can predict epileptic seizures.* He paused. *I want you to use this paperweight to smash the screen.*

What?

I want you to smash your tablet screen. To punctuate what we have done here. The Japanese have a word for recognizing the beauty of broken things. I bet you didn't know that.

I held the paperweight and imagined bringing it down on the screen. Shattering the immaculate glass. The tablet wasn't mine, it belonged to the *WA*, but I felt protective of it somehow. We had been through a lot together. I pulled my lips between my teeth, wondering whether I could do it. Everything, I reminded myself, was either coming out of, or going into, nothingness. I was due an upgrade anyway.

It's OK, Keith nodded.

I lifted my hand in the air and brought it down towards the bottom of the screen. A crack appeared diagonally, from one end to the other. The point I had struck had shattered, making a latticed shape like a spider's web. I slid both objects on to the table in front of me. I felt breathless, exhilarated. Keith reached over and lifted the tablet from his desk. Tiny shards of glass fell like ashes. He ran his finger across the screen and it lit up, light scattering and bleeding between the cracks.

See, he said. *It still works!*

He handed it back to me.

Will I get another? I asked, euphoric.

Oh no, he replied.

Oh, I said.

I tucked the ruined device beneath my arm. It pulled against the fabric of Mia's dress. I understood it was time to leave.

Oh and Ingrid, Keith said, as I stood to go. *You have something in your teeth.*

~~~~~

That evening I received a message on my shattered tablet. I would be getting twenty-four hours of Land Leave the following week. I had not been off the ship for eight months. The message came when I was already in bed. I immediately messaged Mia to ask if she had been given Land Leave. She told me she had not. I messaged Ezra to ask if he had been given Land Leave. He told me he had not. I had no one else to message. I closed my eyes and listened to the ocean to tune the thought out.

When I opened my eyes I wasn't sure what time it was. Outside it was dark, which made me feel an extreme sense of dread, and so I got out of bed and switched on the main light in my cabin, and then the little wall light. I got back into bed but it was still not light enough, so I got up again and switched on the bathroom light as well, and wedged open the door with my chair. I turned the brightness up on my tablet to one hundred per cent. I propped it up against my pillow, a square of burning white. It reminded me of the SAD lamp I'd once received as a gift, how I'd sip coffee in the morning, its blank and robotic face beside me. My tablet, I thought, was more effective. Not at loosening up my dopamine, which was fixed in place, but at providing me with a general sense of comfort and wellbeing. Lying in bed, I kept moving my finger across it so it didn't go to sleep. The

41

cool of the glass against my finger calmed me, a motion like weaving. Eventually I started feeling tired, my finger still stroking the screen. I woke to a room flooded with light.

~~~~~~

A few days later, my manicurist set arrived. Inside a white plastic clip-fasten box I found several different colours of nail varnish and a top coat. Nail varnish remover. A small, zipped purse containing clippers, cuticle removers, an electronic filer/buffer with several attachments, plus a nail brush. There was also a fake rubber hand and a set of acrylic nails. I sat cross-legged on my bed and placed all the items in front of me, experiencing a slightly vertiginous feeling as I did so. I checked my tablet for modules, navigating with some difficulty around the parts of the screen that no longer worked. There were two mandatory modules and ten optional. I began with Intro to Manicures.

In the video, a woman in a black suit was sitting at a clinical metal table. A disembodied hand remained stationary in front of her, the arm extending beyond the screen. Laid out on the table were all of the tools I had been given and more. It felt like seeing an advert for a Christmas present and knowing you were going to get it.

The woman began by stressing the importance of hygiene, explaining how to moisten a cotton-wool swab with disinfectant and use a gentle sweeping motion from wrist to fingertip to clean the customer's hand. She suggested miming this procedure on the rubber hand, since cotton wool and disinfectant are not included in the prep set. I did as I was told, first on the outer side of the hand, and then, more gently, on the underside.

After hygiene came nail shaping and cuticle management. I practised on my own left hand, filing my fingernails into a pleasing squared oval and buffing them till they shone. Peeling away the cuticles in dry, grey curls. My right hand looked drab and weary in comparison.

But coating the nails in varnish was my favourite bit, dragging the brush along the nail, the wet absoluteness of the colour. I felt my world narrow to the hand, and then the finger, and finally just the nail. My breathing became more shallow, less frequent. Recalibrating to what I needed. When I had finished I took a photograph of them to send to Mia.

I cleared away the kit, leaving the white plastic box on my dressing table. The air smelled of vanity and chemicals, which made a change from its usual smell of stale air and stasis. I sat down on the floor. The room felt small and empty, with no jobs left to do. I found myself wishing Ezra was with me. I thought about the soft swell of his stomach and pictured myself wrapping my arms around him, hugging him and then twisting around, so he was pressed to my back, his arms around my shoulders like the straps of a backpack. I thought it would be a good way to go around the world, with someone latched on to you.

I looked down at my body, I needed a wash. I reluctantly pulled off my clothes, everything except my underwear. I couldn't bear the thought of being fully naked so I just showered with them on. Once I was done, I switched off the water and stepped out, trying to summon the inclination to reach for the towel that was literally inches away from me. I waited until I had tucked it firmly in before wriggling out of my bra, letting my pants fall heavily to the floor. Then I blow-dried my body and my hair until I felt exquisitely and unequivocally dry.

I looked in my cupboard for something to eat but I didn't have anything. Outside the window, I couldn't see any land, though I knew it would be there by morning. I pulled closed the shutter and switched off the light.

Land

I disembarked via the small staff bridge. A few other staffers exited with me, pale-faced and fatigued. Wearing *WA* tracksuits and blinking at the light. Some I'd been on rotation with but most I didn't recognize. There was an unspoken understanding Land Leave was to be enjoyed alone and once we crossed the bridge we all went our separate ways.

I stepped on to the land but it still felt as though I was walking on water. The ground did not make the same accommodations as liquid, hard and flat and uncompromising, yet somehow it felt less solid than the sea. I stood still, waiting for my body to steady. I knew the feeling of being at sea would never really leave me, not by then, but I waited a moment anyway. I didn't turn around to look at the *WA* but I felt the mass of it behind me. It was like sleeping next to a body heavier than your own, a weight rolling you from the opposite side of the mattress.

I'd never been to that part of Spain before but the heat felt familiar. The dock was lined with food and drink vendors, quickly assembled tents stocked with tchotchkes and knock-off designer belts. A woman wearing a pink visor and a T-shirt featuring a drawing of a sleeping cat and a slogan exclaiming *Nope!* beneath it crossed my path. She was carrying a cooler filled with shaved ice and soft drinks. I shouted at her and she turned around and walked towards me.

I dragged some change from my pocket, the wrong currency, paying her far too much for a single drink. She studied the silver and copper coins then handed me a can of Fanta, before walking away while shaking her head. I pulled back the tab and felt the pressure release. The bubbles caught in my throat and for a second I couldn't breathe.

I walked until I was surrounded by white buildings, until I could no longer hear or smell the sea. I paused in a narrow street, sweating beneath my clothes. I was still wearing my tracksuit. I continued on, the flannel fabric occasionally making contact with my skin, the sweat fastening it to my body, until I saw a small shop displaying woven bags and straw hats and novelty snorkels. The air conditioning blasted me as I stepped inside and walked towards the clothing at the back.

There were a few options. Cut-off denim shorts and T-shirts stitched with anchors. Swimsuits and bikinis. Dresses hanging from the walls, all white, linen and floor-length. I picked one with thin straps and an elasticated bust and took it to the changing room. It made my skin look more brown and my shoulders seem smaller. I found a black hair tie on the floor and threw forward my head to use it. When I stood up and faced the mirror I looked like an almost completely different person. A woman wearing a white dress and no make-up, hair away from her face. I practised smiling in the mirror. Emerging from the changing room, I picked up one of the woven bags, a large, flat, round one, the size of a small bicycle wheel, plus a pair of enormous tortoise-shell sunglasses, and paid for everything at the counter. Outside, I stuffed my tracksuit, change and credit card into the bag, and put on my sunglasses. I felt sweat evaporate from my skin.

I continued down streets at random, passed buildings shaded fractionally different colours, mustard, apricot, copper. Overhead was vined with telephone wires and electricity cables, occasionally with paper lanterns or parasols. The air smelled like salt, not sea salt but more like cooking, like skin. I heard music coming from somewhere, from a bar nearby. Music, I thought. I like music.

It was ten o'clock in the morning, but inside the bar was pleasantly dark. There were wooden shelves filled with terracotta ashtrays and bronze icons of saints I could not name. There was a leg of cured ham hanging beside the bar. I sat at a table near the entrance, opening a damp newspaper that had been left behind. I couldn't understand the writing but I stared at the photographs. After a few minutes a man appeared at my side.

I asked for coffee, breakfast and a small glass of vermouth. He arranged his face neutrally and enquired as to what kind of breakfast I would like. I told him, *Anything*. Before he walked away, I asked him if he wouldn't mind turning up the volume. He rolled his eyes which I took to mean he was happy to. A few minutes later the sound of decades-old dance music surged through the space. I closed my eyes and listened to the lyrics, about love and money, trying to listen past them, to the instrumentation, the strange choices, a trumpet, an errant snare.

When I opened my eyes my drinks were in front of me. I knocked back the vermouth then stirred cream and sugar into the coffee, sipping it slowly. The man came back with my breakfast, broken eggs over potatoes, and I made a V with my fingers, pointing at both the vermouth and coffee, demonstrating I wanted more. He barely nodded and walked away. I covered the eggs in salt and pepper, mixed them into the potatoes. I found myself chewing to the beat. More coffee and vermouth arrived. I drank them only after I had eaten. When I finished I paid at the bar then stepped out into the sun.

The street was busier than when I had left it. People moved through it with a languid purpose, certain in their right to have no particular destination in mind. I caught sight of a group of tourists, possibly passengers from the *WA*, and decided to follow them. They would know more about where we were and what we were supposed to be doing here, I reasoned.

I kept a little way behind them, ducking into the shops they paused at, squinting at the architectural details they apparently found interesting. There were three men and three women, the men wearing a uniform of camel shorts or wide-fitted trousers, the women in cotton sundresses in ice-cream colours, speaking what was potentially

49

German. Their skin was tender and pink and I felt something I could not distinguish, somewhere between sympathy and contempt.

We cut through an alley which opened up into a large plaza with a fountain at its centre and I felt relieved to be at a kind of landmark, no longer having to follow a group. I left them taking photographs of themselves in front of some stained-glass windows and walked the perimeter of the square before approaching the fountain, removing my shoes to dip my feet into the shallow water. My feet were red and pockmarked from my trainers. They bloated beneath the water.

I twisted my neck to see what was around me. A pale grey building flanked with colourful flags, which I suspected might be an art gallery. It seemed like such a thoroughly normal thing to do. I stepped out of the fountain and walked towards it, trainers in one hand, leaving a trail of increasingly ill-defined footprints in my wake.

I put my shoes on before heading inside and bought myself a ticket. It was perhaps ten minutes before I realized I was still wearing my sunglasses, which is why I couldn't see very well. I balanced them on top of my head in a way that made me feel like a very rich actress. The gallery felt aggressively modern, blue plastic sculptures in the shape of curled ribbons, carved marble faces sticking out from the walls. A huge white room with a tree growing out of the ground. I paused at the descriptions but couldn't bring myself to actually read them. I was finding the layout very confusing. I visited a small exhibition of photography, black and white images I had a feeling I had already seen or possibly even dreamt about or personally experienced. It began feeling like a conspiracy and I made up my mind to get out, but I didn't want to leave until I had visited the gift shop.

The gift shop was excellent and had more energy than the tree room or the photos or the clean, arched architecture many times over. There were books on life drawing and tote bags with the gallery's name and erasers made up like monochromatic colour palettes. I bought a cushion cover with a picture of *The Birth of Venus* and a book on David Hockney. By the time I was finished I felt breathless with overstimulation and in need of a drink. I walked back across the plaza to a restaurant with clean-looking tables beneath a low canvas canopy.

As soon as I sat down, a waitress appeared. She asked if I was eating and I lied instinctually, agreeing that I was. I ordered a pint of lager and hooked my foot around the leg of a chair at an empty neighbouring table, dragging it towards me and putting both my feet up on it. I drank my beer while pretending to look at the menu, and when the waitress approached me I said, *Still deciding!* After I had finished my beer I ordered another, and then another.

A family of four split a pan of paella in front of me, and I stared at the wife/mother, stared at her in a way I hope she took to be unfriendly. She caught the wrist of her husband, whispering something in his ear, and he turned to look at me. I beamed back at him, a woman wearing a white dress and no make-up. He said something to her, something reasonable, which made her look deflated and hurt, then he looked at me again, smiling apologetically. I raised my palm in his direction to show that I understood, his wife was hysterical, then resumed staring at her when he turned away. She didn't say anything to him again. Their children did not turn around.

I grabbed the arm of the waitress when she walked past me and told her I would like the bill. She said something like, *So you won't be eating?* and I ignored her. I paid and stood up, stumbling only slightly, steadying myself on the table. The waitress and the wife were looking at me, their horror plain. I thought, I would fucking kill you in a fight, I would rip you limb from limb. Then I moved away, putting one foot in front of the other.

My head was pounding and I felt sick. I kept walking. Eventually I found another square, no fountain this time, but it had a monument at the centre, the kind with steps around it. It would do. I sat for a while and watched all the people going by, thinking about the awful unpleasantness of being surrounded by strangers. Before joining the

WA, during moments of directionlessness I'd find myself looking for bins, bins at bus stations, bins in town centres, just ordinary public bins, lingering beside them, comforted by their sour smell. I looked around, hoping to spot one, something a bit more objectively terrible than I was, but I couldn't see any.

A man my age appeared beside me, removing what looked like a diary and a pen from his satchel, then began writing. I noticed he was handsome with a firm body and I dragged myself nearer to him, then, when I was close enough, I took the diary and pen from his hands. I turned to the back page and wrote, *I would like to fuck you.* I placed the diary on the hot stone between us, pushing it towards him and positioning my body in a way I imagined looked alluring. He picked it up and read the message as my hair came loose, collapsing in front of my face. I flipped my head upside down to tie it up once again, pausing a moment so I did not throw up, then slowly sat up, blood pulsing at my cheeks. I turned to gauge his reaction but he had already gone, his satchel disappearing into the crowd. I momentarily considered following him, considered begging him, but I got the feeling he was not the type on whom that would work.

Instead, I lay across the stone ledge, stretched my legs out in front of me, alternately tuning in and out of conversations. The longer I remained there the more drunk I felt. I put a hand to my stomach and concentrated on making it go up and down. I wondered how Mia and Ezra were, what they were doing at that exact moment, whether they were thinking about me.

I must have drifted off because I was woken abruptly by someone sitting down next to me. I twisted around to see if it was the man with the satchel, my field of vision filled by a woman's hand wrapped around the edge of the stone, one of her fingers bound in gauze and the others badly bruised. I wrestled myself up, noticing my dress was already filthy.

Hey, I said to her.

Hello, she said back, in a Spanish accent.

Do you speak English? I asked.

A bit, she said.

How did you do that? I pointed to her finger.

My son, she said. *My son slammed it in the door.*

What! I yelped, shocked.

Oh no, she said. *Not like that. No, it wasn't his fault. I was shouting at him and his sister to quieten down. They were running around me, screaming like they do. So I follow them as they ran into the next room, putting my hand like this, in the doorway.*

She demonstrated how she curled her hand around the frame.

And then he slams it to keep his sister away, she said. *It breaks my finger.*

Did it hurt? I asked.

Yes, she said. *Of course it hurt. It hurt so much I fell to the floor.*

Oh, I said. *I'm sorry.*

It's OK, she said. *It's not your fault. Or my son's.*

I lay back down and thought about what it must be like to be in so much pain you collapse. The woman was still sitting there and I wondered whether I could put my head in her lap, whether if I did, she might stroke my hair the way Mia and Ezra do. She was a mother after all. But before I could properly entertain the notion she was met by two kids, presumably her children, in their very early teens. They ran towards her and she stood up, hugging them with one arm each. They walked off talking in Spanish. They were extremely loud and I thought about covering my ears. Instead, I sat myself up again, feeling suddenly keen to do something, to make something of my day. It was still very bright, late afternoon, sunset hours away. My head still hurt but it also felt clear and alert. I remembered Mia telling me about a drink I had to try, red wine and Coke, which was allegedly a thing here. That is what I need, I thought. That is the thing to get me going.

I spotted another group of tourists, unquestionably American. I meandered after them for a bit. They were obviously wealthier, the women wearing dresses in thin, silky fabrics, and the men in pale, loose suits. They took me out of the square and down a long, palm-tree-lined promenade. They didn't stop at any shops or pause to take in any architectural details. They walked with a determination that suggested they had some kind of reservation, but I was not interested enough to find out where it was. I let them drop me off at the first vaguely wine-bar-looking place we passed.

The bar was furnished with tables made out of barrels and topped with polished wood in various abstract shapes. I chose one at random, sitting down to study the menu. It was quite loud and relatively busy for so early in the evening, and I was wondering whether it was a special bar of some kind when the waiter approached me, already annoyed. I asked for wine and Coke, but he didn't understand what I was saying, so I scrambled across the menu, pointed to Kalimotxo, local speciality. He glowered and removed the menu, and I shouted after him, *Plus water, agua.*

The waiter came back with a highball glass of Kalimotxo, water, and a small plate containing three medium-sized prawns. I forgot to say thank you. The wine/Coke combination was peculiar, rich, sickly and fizzy, but I could see the appeal. The prawns were good, very fresh. The water was disgusting. I decided I couldn't stomach another Kalimotxo so I paid and left, wandering down the promenade, peering into the different bars and restaurants. They were all too overstuffed with people. But then I had a brilliant idea. I would buy a bottle of wine from a shop. I would have a picnic. I was so delighted by my own genius I nearly jumped off the ground.

I turned into a side street, and then another, and then the next one, until at last I happened upon a shop. I walked past the fruit and vege-tables, the fridges filled with chicken and fish, until I reached the alcohol. I'd already started on red wine, I reasoned, and so I should continue.

At the counter, an elderly man served me. I handed him the bottle and he scanned it through. He said something to me in Spanish. I shook my head. He tried again and I still just shook my head. Eventually he said, *Dancing?*

Yes! I said. *Yes, I am going dancing!*

Good, he said, tentatively. *Have fun!*

I will! I replied. *I'm going dancing!*

I picked up the bottle and left the shop to go and drink my wine alone.

I headed back towards the coast, retracing my steps. I had been away from the sea long enough that if I didn't exactly miss it, I felt like I wouldn't mind having it nearby. The journey back felt less frantic, more intuitive, and I enjoyed moving through the settling evening.

At the square, the stone steps were covered with groups on picnic blankets, spread with bread, cheese, cold cuts, olives, wine, and sometimes tea lights. I paused at the scene, trying to figure it out. The dusk made everything seem soft, the surfaces more pliable, the colours less offensively brilliant. I wondered whether I should set up camp there for a bit, maybe even join a group. They seemed so lax and porous, like there was room for me in almost every one. I started a lap of the square, feeling it out. I imagined languidly wandering over, smiling and sitting down, opening my wine and helping myself to their crisps and avocado. But the more I circled, the denser the huddles looked. After a while I grew despondent and resentful, imagined kicking over their boxes of juice, stamping on their tomatoes. I gave up on the idea and continued on my journey back to the port, where there was certainty, where I knew what I was going to get. I opened my wine on the go. I didn't need to sit down to drink.

When I arrived at the sea wall I was pleased to find it notched with steps. I walked about halfway down, concentrating on my footing, then squatted and pressed my back against the concrete. It was still warm from the day. I looked either side of me and noticed a few other people sitting there too, mainly couples, but the occasional person alone. I had about two thirds of my wine left and as much time as I needed to drink it. It was both acidic and sweet. Along the coast I could see the *WA*, far enough that it could have been any ship. I compelled myself to look away, out to the ocean, but my eyes kept wandering back. Instead I studied the bottom half of my dress, the clues it contained from my day, dust from the plaza, egg yolk from my breakfast. I wondered whether this is the benefit of wearing white. I drank more wine and thought about having another nap. I felt the edges of a memory and drank through it. I didn't have to be back on ship until the early hours of the morning.

As the weather cooled, the light faded and I felt a greater sense of urgency to finish the task, to down the bottle. When I stood up I was pleased to find that my head felt disconnected from my neck, my limbs like they were floating. I steadied myself with one arm and used the other to toss the empty bottle into the sea. There was a time when I would have found this act repugnant but by then it very much felt like no big deal. As the bottle flew from my hand I made an animal sound, watching as it landed in the water.

In my mind the shopkeeper's comment surfaced like a prophecy, like a promise that everything could still be all right. Dancing! I grappled up the steps and made my way along the wall, along the seafront parade, until I found another bar. There was something terrible about the coastal bars, their dark kind of chaos. Perhaps it was their precariousness. Inside it was busy and bright and absolutely rammed with tourists. I was shitfaced and filthy and scarcely able to walk. I grabbed hold of strangers' shoulders in order to make my way through and only when I felt a sense of solid resistance did I realize I was at the actual bar and there was a bartender in front of me, waiting for my order.

Vodka, I heard myself say. *Vodka tonic.*

A memory butted into view, the same one from before, just the bottom corner of it. When my drink arrived I snatched it and staggered back into the crowd. There was a DJ and a set of decks and the music was obliviatingly loud. I stood right in front of the speakers, so close I could feel the sound vibrate across my skin. The crowd seemed alternately euphoric and malevolent, as though they could turn on me at any moment, a terrible blank mass. I sipped my drink and swayed, closing my eyes so I didn't have to register anyone looking at me. When I'd finished my drink I hunted empty tables for what remained. I finished off a whisky and Coke, a jar of peanuts, some kind of fruit cocktail with a wedge of pineapple soaked and disintegrating at the bottom. I returned to stand by the speakers but immediately I felt hands on my shoulders and heard a voice telling me I needed to leave. Suddenly I was outside. I kicked the door in frustration, and when the voice asked me not to do that again, I shouted at them not to touch me, though they were not touching me and had made no attempt to do so. I lurched away, still shouting. I shouted at a group of women smoking, shouted at a passing man, demanded to know the time. Astonishingly, he obliged me. I still had five hours left on land.

I craved the comfort of narrow lanes. Feeling my way along building sides, pausing every few minutes to press my face against the walls, to stop myself from being sick, I headed back into the old town. A group of women surrounded me, putting their hands over the exposed bits of my skin, asking me if I was all right. I told them I was fine, told them I would like to be left alone, and I may well have scratched one of them, because eventually they did, they did leave me alone. I kept moving until I saw what looked like a small bed and breakfast. I spent a few minutes struggling to open the door until an elderly woman opened it for me and helped me inside.

I propped myself up at reception and rifled through my bag until I produced my credit card. I remembered the things I bought at the art gallery, a long time ago, and wondered where they had gone. The elderly woman rang up my card and said something indistinct, then moved around the desk and ushered me towards a lift. She came in with me, riding the lift then steering me out of it and into the nearest room. She laid me out on the bed and I was vaguely aware of her removing my trainers. She disappeared then came back with a glass of water. The room would not stop spinning.

I woke up to the sound of something happening. I opened my eyes and registered an unfamiliar hotel room. The walls were cream-coloured and the ceiling was covered with embossed flowers. I was still quite drunk. The clock on the bedside table told me it was 4.30 a.m. I had one hour until I needed to be back on board. Outside the door I could hear the sound of an argument escalating until bodies started slamming against the corridor walls. I couldn't remember locking my door and so I dragged myself out of the bed. I twisted closed the large bronze lock, fastened the chain. I could still hear the argument and it gave me an unpleasantly familiar feeling. I wrung my hands violently then kicked the wall for a bit. When that didn't work I looked around for a glass, found one lying in a wet patch underneath my bed, and took it to the bathroom to fill. I splashed more water on my face and underneath my arms, then dried myself with a towel.

My trainers were waiting at the bottom of the bed and I reluctantly put them back on. I walked towards the window and pulled both sets of curtains open. The street outside was quiet, paved, lit dimly by a single lamp. I wondered where I was. I was not too worried, I always found my way back. I retrieved my tracksuit from the now battered straw bag and pulled it on. The hotel room was not a million miles away from my room aboard the *WA*. It had been a good transitional space.

I went to the bathroom for another glass of water and then I checked I still had my credit card. I dumped the last of the change on the unmade bed and left the stained white dress on the floor like a corpse. I looked around the hotel room, not yet quite ready to leave. I wondered whether the leather document holder contained a menu, whether I could order room service, but I knew I didn't have time. I picked up the telephone from the bedside table, called down to reception, and asked for a cab. As I made my way towards the door I caught sight of myself in the bathroom mirror and I had an idea. Another good idea. I stepped back inside the bathroom and wrapped the fingers of my left hand around the door frame. I pulled back the door with my right hand, as far back as it would go, and then I slammed it.

Sea

Before I started working on the *WA*, at weekends I would wake up mid-afternoon, slow from too much sleep, unable to do much beyond eat toast spotted with Marmite, watch entire television shows, full seasons of them, in one sitting. I'd lie across the worn velvet of a couch inherited from my aunt, propped up with embroidered pillows, scrolling through photographs of old colleagues and classmates, their children and partners, on my phone. I'd jump from website to website, buying sweatshirts and dresses and jumpsuits, only to return them the same week they arrived, often without trying them on. I could structure an entire day around a hypothetical trip to the bubble-tea vendor in town, or a walk to McDonald's for Chicken McNuggets. I'd never quite manage to leave the flat on those days, the evening drawing determinedly in. Like watching the lift doors close, an engagement ring disappear down the drain, nature just following its course, and me, sitting on my sofa, observing it.

The morning after I went to Spain, I woke with that same listless feeling. A throbbing head and hand. A floor blanketed by pistachio shells, tissues and blood. A sad pile of unclean clothes. It took me a few moments to remember what had happened. I lifted my left hand to my face. My fingers were bound in blood-soaked toilet paper, swollen and curled in on themselves, like prey animals, hiding. I considered my options before using my right hand to drag my tablet from beneath my bed, logging a sick day and booking an appointment at the hospital. The pain tuned in and out while I dressed myself clumsily, attempting to scrape handfuls of tissue paper and pistachio shells into the bin. I knew I had broken one, if not two, fingers, and I worried about what that might mean, work-wise. I wondered whether I regretted what I'd done, but it felt like regretting hair loss or catching a cold. It was beyond my control.

The hospital was on one of the lowest decks. Ordinarily, I'd take the stairs because I like to get a sense of the depth, but I was too tired, too hungover, and so I headed for the lifts. As the car moved down I felt the familiar sensation of compression, the air thickening and my ears popping. I felt the pressure in my fingers too, like they might shatter, like they might split even further apart.

The hospital didn't look like a real hospital because of course it was not. It was more like a staged infirmary or mock ward. After a long time waiting, drinking too-cold water from conical paper cups, I was called over to see the nurse. She pulled up my records before asking me what I was here for. I presented her with my hand, placing it on the table between us. I hadn't bothered changing the tissue paper because I was too scared to discover what was underneath without immediate medical supervision.

What happened here? she asked.

It got caught, I said. *It got caught in a door.*

She made a sound to tell me she was listening without judgement.

I think it's broken, I said.

She paused for what seemed too long. *Well let's take a look, shall we?* she said.

She cut away the tissue paper, now stiff and brown with dried blood, using a small pair of scissors, removing the sections which remained matted to my flesh with water-soaked cotton swabs. Beneath, the flesh was purple, with pink veins of clotted blood. My finger was three times its usual size, like a cartoon finger, and I tried moving it but the pain referred from my hand to behind my eyes, so I stopped.

Well the ring finger is definitely broken, she said. *But the others are fine. What rotation are you on?*

Gift shop, I said. *But I'm finishing soon.*
Aha, she replied. *And the next one?*
Manicurist.
Well, she smiled. *Isn't that ironic.*

She walked out of the room and left me alone, contemplating its stark whiteness. The empty countertops offered no respite, the white cupboards along the wall, their blank, indifferent faces. There was so much unoccupied space, filled only by harsh, intrusive light. I felt like a microorganism marooned in a Petri dish, being studied for signs of life. The nurse returned holding a syringe and a vial of pale yellow liquid.

This might hurt, she said.
This, I said, lifting my hand, *already hurts.*

She smiled, half-patient, half-passing the time, and began handling my ring finger, looking at it all the way round. She injected the vial directly into my finger, little punctures and small expulsions across the length and circumference of it, at seemingly random intervals. I imagined the yellow liquid expanding beneath my skin, channels coalescing and mapping the pain. Once finished, she lowered my hand on to the table and watched it. I followed her lead. I wondered whether I should be able to see some kind of transformation.

After a moment I felt my hand cool. I looked at my finger, its pulverized flesh, realizing what a grotesque aberration it was, surrounded by sterile, stainless steel. I felt embarrassed to have brought it here, a dog dragging a dead bird into the lounge. And it wasn't just my finger or even my hand that was the anomaly, it was me. I had been on land too long and it lingered on me, remained in the alcohol, fat and sugar that travelled through my veins, in the sunlight that had browned my skin, the nicotine and dust stiffening my hair.

The nurse began applying an antiseptic-smelling cream to my finger, gently massaging it into the skin. I noticed with a small jolt of pride that my nail varnish remained intact, the clean arc at the nail bed curved like a smile, the glossy top coat that had prevented it from chipping. I imagined my customers looking at their own nails after I had attended to them, the little boost it might give them. How they might show their friends and perhaps even recommend me.

The nurse slotted my finger into a blue sponge cast. It reminded me of the material we sometimes wrapped the crystalware in, and the thought that a part of my body could be seen as fragile and requiring of as gentle handling as, say, a long-stemmed sherry glass, or a reed-diffusing scent bottle, was even a little moving. Once the cast was taped up, she handed me a roll of surgical tape, telling me to tighten it as the swelling reduced. She also gave me three plastic pillboxes, one for the inflammation, one for the pain, and some antibiotics, just as a precaution.

You be careful, she said, discharging me.

~~~~~

Back in my cabin I uncovered my porthole and lay down across my bed, still fully clothed, the light pouring through in burnt yellow streaks. It was still a little rocky and I rolled gently sideways with each wave, occasionally engaging my stomach muscles to remain in place. After a while I dragged myself to the bathroom to urinate dark, dehydrated piss and then I returned to my position on the bed.

To pass the time I imagined what was going on elsewhere on the ship. I thought about the sunloungers lined up like caskets, the elegant parcels of feta and spinach served in the tapas bar. Periodically these scenes would be ruptured by old memories spilling in, the scarf my husband brought me from a work trip to France, how he would eat everything with a large spoon.

Often after Land Leave I felt the need to zip up, to be totally contained within my own skin, entirely alone in my shame. But when I started feeling hungry and, later, very hungry, I reluctantly messaged

Mia. I went to unlock the door, knowing she would let herself in without knocking, knowing it would not occur to her to do otherwise.

So I'm not even going to ask, she said, noticing my hand within seconds of seeing me.

It's nothing, I grunted. *It got caught in a door.*

Mm hmm.

I shuffled over so she could lie down beside me. She tucked one arm beneath my neck and pushed the hair from my face with her other, stroking my head as we watched the shadows on the ceiling move.

You smell disgusting, she said, indifferently, without judgement. Like, this milk is off.

We lay for a while in silence, and I was grateful that she did not need to fill up the space with sound. Sometimes I would move my eyes sideways to watch the insistent protrusions of her cheeks, the heavy hoods of her eyes.

I had a dream about you once, I said to her.

Oh yeah, she replied.

Yeah. I had a dream you stretched the skin of your belly and folded it around me, lifting me up and carrying me around like a pre-partum baby. I woke up feeling very relaxed.

People are always telling me their dreams about me, she remarked. *And honestly I wish they would not.*

We continued lying there for perhaps an hour before Mia announced she would wash me. She helped me to my feet, then out of my trainers and socks, my tracksuit, my underwear. I waited naked in the centre of my cabin as she switched on the shower. I wondered how I should stand, should I relax a knee or cock a hip. I didn't mind being naked so long as there was someone else around.

Come on, she said. *Let's get you clean.*

She removed the showerhead from its handle and gestured for me to step inside.

Can you get this wet? she asked, pointing at my hand.

I don't know, I replied. *The nurse didn't say.*

Well then, she said. *Let's assume you can't.*

I held my arm straight out in front of me and Mia sprayed me with water while I rubbed soap into my skin. I couldn't wash my hair with one hand, and so I held the showerhead while she worked shampoo into my scalp, then rinsed it out, conditioned the hair and rinsed again. She wrapped one of the big towels around me, then fixed one of the smaller towels around my head.

I'll dry your hair for you, she said.

Will you? I could hear the vulnerability in my own voice.

Of course, she said. *I know how you like to be dry.*

I sat in the chair and Mia stood behind me. It made me think of the days when I used to visit hairdressers. The whole carnival of it. How they would bring me a cocktail and a magazine, ask about my holidays. I would sit in the salon chair and think, I can be any kind of person.

Once my hair was dry, Mia helped me into my pyjamas. She told me to get into bed while she tidied up my room, picking up the rest of the pistachio shells and the bloodied tissues, plus other things I hadn't noticed, bobby pins, paper clips, chocolate-bar wrappers, clumps of hair. I imagined her as a child, taking care of Ezra. Their parents were both research biologists, working for a pharmaceutical company, and they weren't around much. Mia told me she learned to boil an egg aged eight. By the time she was ten her parents would ask her how to use the different settings on the washing machine. She told me so in a way that suggested she was very proud of this information.

When she'd finished cleaning up the floor, she changed my bedsheets, occasionally requesting I roll this way or that, never requiring me to actually remove myself from the mattress. She put my old bedding and damp towels in a cotton bag, told me she would drop them off at the laundry service and come back with clean ones. Before she left me, she told me to close my eyes, said my face had gone grey. She would be back in a bit.

When she was gone my eyes opened by themselves. My cabin looked fresh and renewed. Mia had done a good job tidying it up and it made me feel like I too had the potential to be good and clean. But without Mia in it, the room's glow seemed to fade almost immediately. I thought about my old apartment, the hours I spent waiting for my husband to get home from work, how he mostly worked late. Evenings lying out across the sofa, the television occasionally on in the background, for company. Though mostly I wouldn't switch it on, would just sit bathed in the silent, sea-green light. I don't think I was bored. I was just anxious for his presence, my heart beating eagerly, waiting for him to come home.

I pulled myself back into the present. I wanted things to be different. The dark of the cabin held the promise of renewal, a screen fading to black and another episode beginning. I took my pills as the nurse had instructed me and it felt like the swelling in the fingers had improved, if only slightly. Shortly afterwards, Mia came back, moving with a subtle air of importance. It made me feel very protective of her.

Ezra's joining us soon, she said. *And he's bringing food.*

She sat at the foot of my bed and we both waited. Every now and then I noticed her gaze fall to my hand and something inscrutable pass across her face.

Are you sure you're OK? she said eventually, staring straight ahead.

I'm fine, I replied. A sentence I'd never been able to deliver convincingly.

When Ezra arrived, he knocked just once, a soft and flat sound. Mia opened the door to discover him standing with polystyrene boxes stacked up to just below his face. He placed the boxes very gently on the desk and Mia helped dismantle the structure, taking them down and soberly announcing their contents. Turmeric cod. Hispi cabbage. Hawaiian pizza. Potato laksa. Salted green beans. Goat cheese ravioli. Once they were all spread out, Mia clapped her hands, an unusually girlish gesture which she seemed immediately to regret, and asked me what I had to eat them with.

Climbing out from beneath the bedsheets, I looked inside the cupboard where I kept the various bits of tableware that had found their way from restaurants and cafes into my possession. Nothing seemed quite right for the occasion. Eventually I just dragged everything out. There were a couple of dinner plates and side dishes, some round and some square, a number of bowls in different sizes, and an array of arcane utensils, steak knife, cheese slice, miniature ladle, salad fork. We made do, sitting widthways along the bed, like a sleepover. After we'd finished eating we watched an episode of *The X-Files*. It was about a man who killed people to eat the cancerous parts of their bodies. There was a bit in which his mum says he was horribly bullied, and if he killed anyone, that was because they deserved to die. There was another bit where the cancer-eating man sheds his body like a snake shedding its skin, then Scully finds out she has cancer, and that the man wants to eat her because of this. Then we watched an episode of *Frasier* where they all go camping and one of them reads *Walden*. It made me wonder when I had last read a book, but before I could follow the thought through, Ezra interrupted me.

When are you back in work? he asked.

Tomorrow, I said. *Last shift in the shop.*

He looked vaguely startled. *That went fast.*

What's your next rotation? Mia asked.

Manicurist, I said, eyes on the screen. Martin was telling Frasier a scary story. He made a joke about Frasier's sleeping bag being soaked in urine. *But this time I'm managing.*

You're the manager? Mia said slowly. *Have you ever managed?*

First time, I shrugged. *How about you?*

I just moved over to the pizza place, she reminded me. *The one on the third deck.*

Free pizza, though?

Yeah, she said, resignedly. *Free pizza.*

We moved on to an episode of *Cheers* I'd seen many times before. Pain flickered from my hand to my elbow. I felt bloated and hungry at the same time. Mia kept looking over at me. I could see her getting herself worked up the way I used to watch my mother frantically cleaning the house. Something accumulating, ready for release. It gave me the same dark feeling that I used to have then, that something was wanted from me and I had unwittingly failed to deliver it.

I'm not sure about this, Mia announced.

About what?

Management, she said. *The programme. It's obviously too much for you.*

She lifted my hand from where it rested on my stomach, holding it in front of my face. An offending item. I watched her move it through the air, proving her point. I didn't mind other people manipulating my appendages. They generally did a better job of taking care of my body than I could.

Am I the only one who is going to acknowledge that she is not coping, she said, not to me, not to Ezra, not to anyone really. *I think she really needs to consider whether this programme thing is worth persevering with.*

What do you mean? It's nothing to do with the programme?

Leave her alone, Ezra sighed, taking my hand and placing it gently back on to my torso. Mia glowered at him. She looked like she was going to cry. Ezra gazed back, both anxious and sleepy. I knew I had to intervene.

Does anyone fancy a game of Families? I offered.

Ezra immediately perked up, remembering that it was his turn to be the baby. Mia still looked worked up, but then she shrugged, blinked, and the cloud passed.

We only played a short game. We sat Ezra on the floor and he pointed out all of the things he wanted us to show him. We brought them over to him, so he could look at them or feel them or throw them to the ground. He pointed at a soup spoon and turned it over in his hands. He pointed at a picture frame, a commemorative photo of the *WA*, and immediately dropped it. He pointed at a pen and drew all over his face. After that we decided enough was enough. We all had shifts the next morning.

Ezra wanted to carry on but Mia and I dragged him up and pushed him towards the door, half-making a game of it. There was a strange moment in which it seemed like he wouldn't break character, like we might push him out into the corridor, out into the world, and he would remain a baby, palsied and non-verbal, no more than eleven months old. The thought made me panic. Perhaps one day we would be playing and we wouldn't be able to stop. He tilted his head to one side, exaggeratedly cute. His limbs were floppy, dead weights. The naked need of it was monstrous, a terrible gravitational pull. When I couldn't stand it any more, I slapped him, just once, but hard, using my good hand.

That's enough, I whispered. *Stop it.*

He cradled his face. Beneath his hand his cheek looked pink and tender. I waited for remorse but it never came.

I'm sorry, he said. *I'm sorry.*

I didn't dare look at Mia for her reaction, but I could feel her behind me, observing. After a while Ezra picked up his jacket from the back of my chair and went wordlessly away, still clutching his reddened cheek. I turned to face Mia, braced for her indignation.

Don't worry about that, she said, tartly. *He deserved it.* Her allegiance was somehow worse.

She arranged the polystyrene boxes into two piles, the bottoms and the lids, slotting them neatly on top of each other. She stacked the plates and bunched the cutlery together. With the polystyrene boxes in her hands, she opened the door with her foot.

Presume you're going to wash those? she asked, nodding towards the plates.

I'll do them in the bathroom basin.

Well make sure you do, she said. *I'll see you soon.*

When she left I noticed I didn't feel as alone as I had before, though I unquestionably was.

<center>~~~~~</center>

Usually at the end of a rotation there was some kind of fanfare. Small, plain cakes stolen from the crew mess. Sugary spritzers in plastic cups. Sweet, sticky things to see you off. I never outwardly wanted the fanfare but I was also scared of what it might mean if there wasn't any. What I really wanted was to be the reluctant star of a party thrown in my honour. And I did feel there should be some acknowledgement this time, more so than the others, on account of the exceptional work I had done. I had re-merchandised the cosmetics, allowing greater footfall for the moisturizers and hydrating hair products, after I'd heard customers complain the sea air dries them out. I had created a new taxonomy for the phone covers, accounting for both phone model and cover brand. I had arranged the loose gold neck chains from the palest gold through to the darkest, in a way that made me, and I assume others, think of the sound a glockenspiel makes when you drag the mallet from one end to the other.

I had done inventive, meaningful work that had come from a place of genuine care. When I compared what I had achieved during my relatively brief tenure at the gift shop to the likes of Zach or the new girl whose name I had made a point of not remembering, it was actually laughable, I had to laugh. And walking to complete my final shift, I did laugh. I laughed the whole way there.

I felt light of foot walking over, though when I saw the shop's front door, I got the familiar but unnameable sensation of melancholy and regret. It took a few moments to get myself together before I remembered to smile and do my rounds, to transform anxiety into excitement.

After a spell behind the counter, I started wondering what time it was, how long I had been there and how long I had left. Being on the

WA had given me a complicated relationship with time. It was so elemental to the project, to our lives. The number of hours in a shift, the number of weeks in a rotation, the number of years at sea. The constant clock-watching, the calendar-watching, a focus so intense it stopped meaning anything, like staring at a very bright light until you are blinded. I could work shifts noticing literally every minute pass, but by the end it felt like I had been there no time at all. My days went by in a flash. In a way, minutes passed felt like minutes saved, like proof of more to come. The inevitability of time continuing and the scale always balanced between future and past. I felt like I was mostly in credit. And at least when I was working I was doing something substantial. I was producing. The time I was not on shift felt more like time wasted, time I considered dead.

I looked at my finger, the sponge canoe that carried it, and felt a deep sense of resignation. The pain had somehow got worse overnight, or perhaps just more articulate. The pain of bones rearranging and healing. I felt a strong desire for the whole world to just get on with things. To distract myself from the wound, I wiped down the till area though it wasn't unclean at all. Then I did a lap of the shop, as if marching in honour of my own legacy. I wondered how different my experience at the nail salon would be.

About halfway through my day, I was confident there would be no fanfare, my efforts had been in vain. I decided to create my own kind of celebration by throwing myself even more vigorously into my work, to go out on a bang. I scanned the shop for the wealthiest- and most suggestible-looking customers, eventually identifying a woman in her late sixties wearing what appeared to be a real fox-fur coat and too many strings of pearls to be of completely sound mind. A large Chanel handbag hung from the crook of her arm. When I got close to her, I could see her earlobes lined with diamond-studded earrings, a strange shade of yellow eyeshadow caked in the corners of her eyes. There was something about her that made me want to close my eyes and sleep for a year.

One thing about working in the gift shop that could be pretty annoying was that the shop was where the customers tended to die. They'd be perusing the aisles, sliding sunglasses on to their faces or wrapping stoles around their shoulders, looking at themselves in the mirror, and they'd just drop. It was usually the long-term passengers, the ones who had long since given up on day trips. It was as if they had some internal homing device, drawing them to the gift shop, its bright objects and heavily perfumed smells. Like cats finding a safe corner in which to die. There were people trained to deal with this. We'd call them and they'd come in to clean up the mess. The woman with the yellow eyeshadow didn't look like a typical death risk but you never knew.

May I help you with anything? I asked her.

I don't think so, she replied. *I'm just happy having a look. I'm just looking at things.*

In order to demonstrate her agency she began fingering the cashmere scarves, the blood-red gloss of her fingernails moving violently against their muted pastels. The woman reminded me of Christmas, the expense and inelegance. I persevered though I wasn't certain why.

Have you seen our new line of Inuit boots? I said. *Toscana shearling lined with rabbit fur. Satin laces. And they come in a number of different colourways.*

Not for me, I'm afraid. I'm really just looking. She cleared her throat. An ineffectual bid to compel me away from her.

How about one of our bangles? I continued. *We've got some Turkish silver in at the moment.*

She shook her head and half-smiled. I watched her trace her fingertips against the scarves again, not even bothering to look at the price sticker. She left the scarves and moved towards the electronics. She really was just looking. The vulgarity of being in a shop and not actually shopping was making me feel sick and for a moment I thought I might punch her or, better yet, grab a fistful of her hair and slam her head into a countertop.

Perhaps you might be interested in some of our exclusive WA *merchandise?* I said, following her. *We've got some excellent rainproof coats and leather-bound journals. Or might I interest you in some of our new room fragrances? Perhaps something sweet? Goat-milk candy? Lavender jelly? Honeydew mochi?*

She turned to face me, evidently exasperated.

What I would like, she said, not unkindly, *is to be just left alone. Is that OK? To be left alone to browse, please?*

She walked away from me towards the perfumes. I watched the small glass bottles filled with clear and golden liquids and it began making sense to me why people would come to the gift shop to die. The neat aisles and products all lined up like cemetery rows. The same cool calm.

She picked up a bottle in the shape of a skyscraper and spritzed it on her inner forearm. She waited for a moment and then leaned in to sniff. She did this a few more times, selecting a bottle in the shape of a diamond, a bottle in the shape of a love heart, a bottle in the shape of a woman's disarticulated bust. Each time spritzing further up her arm, and always waiting a moment before sniffing. There was something undeniably adept about how she carried on, switching arms when she'd run out of space. The more I watched her, the more her proficient little routine gave me a bottomless sensation that felt very much like a scream.

She caught my eye and half-smiled again, which I took as my invitation to approach her. When I was near enough I moved my face very close to hers and in a low whisper I said, *What the fuck is your problem?* At that moment Zach marched into the centre of the room, parading a wheeled table topped with a multi-tiered cake and a bottle of champagne. I turned away from the woman and the perfume she wasn't planning to buy and walked towards Zach thinking, today has felt almost exactly like my wedding.

~~~~~

A week into my new rotation, I had another appointment with Keith. I had started organizing my time around our meetings, and while I rarely knew what day of the week it was, or even what month of the year, I knew how many days had passed since my last meeting, how many days until my next. I would wake with the sick feeling of anticipation, would have to sit up straight and sip water in bed until it passed. I'd get myself ready with a nervy kind of joy.

I began wearing more make-up to the meetings. I suppose this was because I wanted Keith to feel like he would have sex with me, if it ever came down to it. I'd press my face with milk-fragranced powder, line my lips with matte red pencil. I'd curl my eyelashes then coat them with a thick layer of mascara. I combed my hair so it looked straight and flat, quaintly obedient. I always felt particularly vulnerable after exercising precision with my make-up, like presenting a delicate art project to a parent or teacher, wanting approval and the promise it will never break. I wore Mia's fitted black dress again, remembering Keith complimenting it previously. I wanted him to know I was taking on board everything he was saying. I was being the best me I could be.

In the waiting room I saw the same familiar faces. The man with the mole. Kai, with her Chardonnay-scented hair. I looked around for Madeleine but she wasn't there. I wondered whether she had dropped out or just been seen before me. Whether there was any meaning in the order of appointments. I always seemed to be in the middle, which I supposed made sense. I folded my hands in my lap, tried to arrange them in a way which hid the sponge cast. I'd peeked beneath it that morning. My finger was less swollen but more purple, in places even slightly black. It looked like it had just died and I couldn't imagine it healing. I practised hanging my hand to my side, tucking it slightly beneath my chair and out of sight. The receptionist called my name.

Keith looked pleased to see me. He wasn't just trying to look pleased to see me, he really was. Not many people could tell the difference but I could. He sipped coffee and looked pleased.

Take a seat, Ingrid, he said, reaching his hand across the desk. I did as I was told, having finally remembered to wait.

How have you been?

I've been well, I said. I thought about my new rotation, managing two people, both more experienced than me. I thought about bringing it up. Surely he would already know. Mia was right, I had realized after our argument, to my great irritation. It must be part of the programme. I weighed up the pros and cons of mentioning it myself versus waiting for Keith to say something, when he interrupted my train of thought.

Ingrid, he said. I liked it when he said my name. *Is there something you would like to tell me?*

There is. I took a deep breath. I wanted to sound strong-willed, a serious kind of person. Someone who was competent and up to the challenge. *I've been made a manager.*

I know, Keith said. *And I think you know I know. And so I am not sure why you would waste both of our time telling me about that, instead of explaining how you have damaged your hand.*

I blinked. He gazed back at me between sips of coffee. Clear-sighted and efficient. The image of accomplishment. I lifted my hand from my side and deposited it on to his desk. I wanted to shock him.

I was drinking, I said. *And I slammed my hand in a door.*

I watched how he received the information, registering a small eye pop of surprise. I had spoken deliberately, with an air of indifference, with a suggestion of contempt. It made me think of my mother telling me about all the terrible things she had lived through. The sacrifices she had made in order to have me. The confrontational subtext of it.

I didn't know you drink, Keith said. He seemed unmoored, casting around. It made me feel powerful. *Do you drink a lot?*

I don't, I replied. I sounded unusually loose, like I didn't care what he asked me. *I never drink any more.*

He sat up straight. *There must be a reason for that*, he said quickly. I realized I had given him what might amount to ammunition. *Why might that be, Ingrid? Something you have regretted, something that happened while under the influence? A terrible mistake? Maybe you feel you cannot control the drinking?*

I stared at my hand, which was still resting on his desk. A gift I was too guileless to realize was unwanted. I pulled it back into my lap where it belonged.

Interesting. Keith was nodding to himself. *All very interesting. When did you first start drinking?*

I shrugged in a way I hoped seemed casual. *That's not something I want to talk about*, I said.

Keith looked disappointed. But more than that, he looked unimpressed. I tried to think about it in a way that felt rational. It wasn't a big deal. I was calm and loose, very much in control.

But I will talk about it, I added. *If you want me to?*

Please do, he replied. *That is absolutely what I want.*

I nodded. Of course it was.

It started after a bad day at work, I said. *Something had happened with a client. I forget now, but it upset me a lot. I left the office in the middle of the afternoon, went to the nearest bar, ordered a bottle of wine for myself. When I left I could barely walk. I got the bus home and I was sick on the top deck. It was over very quickly.*

When we stopped at a traffic light I saw my husband out the window, sitting across the street at another bus stop. I couldn't believe it. I watched him take out his phone and seconds later I heard my own phone ring, he was ringing me. I badly wanted to answer it, to tell him I was right across the road. But I let it ring out. Watched him put his phone back in his pocket, get on a bus going the opposite direction. I sent him a message saying I was still at work and couldn't talk. He replied saying he was meeting some friends and just wanted to know where I was. I went home and showered, got straight into bed. He came home a few hours later.

Again, Keith said.

I cleared my throat and started over.

I'd been drinking for about three weeks, hiding it from my husband, telling him I had to work late or I wasn't feeling very well. One afternoon something had happened with a client, I forget what it was but it upset me. I left the office in the middle of the afternoon, went to a bar near work, ordered a bottle of wine and a ham panini, then another bottle of wine. When I left I could barely walk, had to hold on to railings, rest against bins. I got the bus home. Not the train or a taxi, because it seemed more undignified to vomit in a train or taxi. In a bus you could just sit on the top deck, lower your head between your legs, and that was that, you were done.

I gave the driver a handful of change and clambered up the stairs. I was sick. It was over very quickly. Oatmeal chunks of bread and pink slivers of ham. We stopped at a traffic light and I moved my hand against the window, making a circle in the steam. Across the road was another bus stop, and sitting at the bus stop was my husband. I couldn't believe it. I started to cry.

I watched him look at the traffic, watched him remove his glasses and clean them with his sleeve. Then I watched him reach into his jacket pocket, take out his phone. I momentarily thought I was going to catch him out, discover him having an affair. He held the phone to his ear and seconds later I heard my own phone ring. I held it in my hand and thought about how badly I wanted to answer it, to tell him I was sad and drunk and right across the road, and would he come and get me, please. But I let it ring out. Watched him put his phone back in his pocket, get on a bus going the opposite direction.

I sent him a message saying I was still at work and couldn't talk. He replied saying he was meeting some friends and just wanted to know where I was. I went home and got straight into bed. He came home a few hours later.

There was a strange greed in Keith's gaze. A bad friend who urges you to do something embarrassing or stupid. *Again*, he smiled. *One more time.*

This is a story about when I first started drinking. I'd been drinking for about three weeks, hiding it from my husband. One afternoon at work I'd had an awful day, something had happened with a client, I forget the details now. *I left the office in the middle of the afternoon, went to a bar near work, ordered a bottle of wine, a ham panini, another bottle of wine. When I left I could barely walk, had to hold on to shopfronts, rest against bins. I got the bus home. Not the train or a taxi, because it seemed more undignified to vomit in a train or taxi. In a bus you could just sit on the top deck, lower your head between your legs, and that was that. So I dropped a handful of change in the little slot and I dragged myself up the stairs. I was sick as soon as I sat down. Oatmeal chunks of bread and pink slivers of ham. I felt desperately sad. I imagined the feel of my husband's arms around me, heard him telling me everything would be fine.*

We stopped at a traffic light and I wiped the window, not really thinking about it, just making a circle in the steam. I could see through it, across the road, there was another bus stop, and sitting at the bus stop was my husband. I couldn't believe it. I started to cry. I watched him look at the traffic, watched him remove his glasses and clean them with his sleeve. Then I watched him reach into his jacket pocket and take out his phone. I momentarily thought I was going to discover him having an affair. He held the phone to his ear and seconds later I heard my phone ring. He was ringing me.

I held my phone in my hand and thought about how badly I wanted to answer it, to ask him to come and get me, please. Take me home. Make me better. But I let it ring out. He put his phone back in his pocket and got on a bus going the opposite direction. I messaged him saying I was still at work and he replied that he was meeting some friends and had just wanted to hear my voice.

I went home, showered, got into bed. He came in a few hours later. I pretended to be asleep and he didn't try to wake me. But the thing is, just before he got on his bus, he looked out across the road and, I swear, he looked right at me. We looked at each other, me from the bus, him from the road, for a second or two. He knew it was me and he knew I'd been lying, but he didn't mention it, not ever.

Keith was slumped low in his chair, his eyes half-closed. I felt breathless, pink-faced. It was almost post-coital.

Good work, Keith said, adjusting his posture. *We're doing good work here.*

Thank you, I said, suddenly shy.

You've got me thinking, he announced. *About your finger, the drinking, not answering the phone to your husband. The things we do to damage ourselves. It's all connected.*

I suppose, I said.

Embracing damage is one of the founding principles of wabi sabi, he said. *Remind me, Ingrid. Are you aware of the Japanese aesthetic tradition of wabi sabi?*

I am.

And so I don't need to explain, he nodded.

I hesitated. *I'd like it if you did*, I said.

I let my vision relax and the room blurred as Keith told me about how everything is coming out of and going into nothingness. It was like listening to a meditation podcast, and for a moment it seemed like he was swelling, inflating like a balloon. That he would fill the whole room and that I would suffocate, pressed tightly against one of the walls. I refocused my sight and the spell was broken, Keith still sitting at the centre of the room, just a normal-sized man. If anything, smaller than I had remembered.

~~~~~

It turned out I enjoyed working in the nail salon. It was a cool, narrow space. A long, banquet-style table sliced the room in half. There were three bamboo stools on either side. At the back of the room were two turgid, high-backed seats with square foot spas tucked underneath them. The room was painted white and it smelled white too, aseptic and corrosive, chemicals that would eat through any stain. Some effort had gone into making the space feel organic, a plastic cheese plant, an artificial Boston fern, and near the entrance a small stone fountain. If you concentrated hard enough, you could make out the dribbling sound of water over the pre-programmed playlist of Laurel Canyon folk or generic lounge.

Sometimes the salon would feel very relaxing to me, like the day spa I used to visit with my friends back when I lived on land. Wrapped in complimentary robes, sipping thin orange soups or lying in saunas until we nearly passed out. And other times the salon felt very stressful to me, redolent of invasive cosmetic procedures, transvaginal scans. Both sensations had their advantages. But mostly it occupied a midpoint between the two, a space intended for work on the self, glossed with the veneer of recreation.

The women I managed were called Rosa and Li. We got on well, they were always very nice to me. I liked how Rosa called me baby, though it disrupted the power differential, and how Li complimented my hair. *So soft*, she would say. *I want to get dressed in it.* During quiet periods I would make us all a cup of chamomile tea, and we would drink it sat around the long table, while I recited my thoughts on how they could be doing things better or at least more efficiently. I thought of myself as the kind of manager ready to *get my hands dirty* and *grab the bull by the horns* and I hoped they did too.

Rosa had been at the salon the longest, and she showed me the ropes, taught me basic French manicures, gels and acrylics, and finally, nail art. Administering manicures with a broken finger was not easy, though I was mostly able to make accommodations. After the salon shut, we would sit in the pedicure chairs, softening our feet in lavender-laced water, and I would ask her questions about balancing the books, reordering supplies. She answered each one while staring straight ahead. When I got home at night, I would watch tutorials on my tablet, sometimes messaging Rosa and Li to clarify a technical point. *No worries if this has to wait until the morning!* I would always sign off, wanting them to know I respected their time.

I took it upon myself to administer the more complicated designs. I'd practise on my pretend hand between shifts, using a toothpick to etch geometric shapes or illustrations. Pressing an acetone-soaked cotton bud against the soft rubber, my work disappeared in an instant. A client asked Rosa for a series of yellow crescent moons against a charcoal-grey sky, and I stepped in, Rosa explaining that I was the most senior member of staff and so she was getting a bargain. Ultimately she seemed quite disappointed with the result but I still felt very proud. Eventually I started working on my own ideas, desert landscapes with the sun setting behind them, tessellating dahlias. I'd bring them in to show Rosa and Li, and they'd compliment me on the concepts, then show me where I was going wrong.

Perhaps my favourite thing about the salon was the concentration required. Like a camera's aperture focusing in on a subject, it felt like my whole world narrowed to the small slope of a stranger's fingernail. It was ornate work, with a kind of timelessness to it, and I felt like part of a lineage of artists working on small canvases. Chinese craftsmen carving patterns into pillboxes made from bone. That guy who painted the *Mona Lisa* on to the end of a pin. Once I'd completed a design I would lean back, my lungs would fill, and the rest of the room would pour into view.

My management responsibilities were less straightforwardly pleasurable. I'd taken only two management modules, one on decision-making and one on delegating work. I found the latter particularly helpful. Instead of saying *Li, wipe the table down* I would say *Li, do you think you could wipe the table down* or *Li, the table needs wiping down*, and after they'd finished I would always tell them what a good job they had done. But mostly I didn't have to resort to these tricks. Rosa and Li would just do what I said because I was in charge. The only time I felt like a fraud was when a customer would ask me a question and I would look blankly at the girls until one of them intervened. But generally I understood why I was the manager and they were not. It was because I was a natural leader.

The nail salon was only open during the day so I had most of my evenings free. Mia was on nights at the pizza parlour and Ezra worked long hours on his new rotation at the photography studio, so we rarely had the opportunity to meet up. Instead, I spent a lot of time alone, taking myself for walks, watching films at the cinema. I was making marginally more money now and I could afford to do a bit more. After a while I got tired of my own company and had the idea to ask Rosa and Li out for dinner. Maybe we could make it a regular thing. I put it to them one afternoon as we shut up shop.

How about a team dinner? I said.

Rosa was dragging a mop across the floor. She dunked it in the soapy water then slapped it back down.

Sure, baby, she said. *Whatever you want.*

<hr>

I arranged the first team dinner at the sushi bar I had been frequenting. It seemed like the sort of place a sophisticated person might take people less ostensibly sophisticated than they were. We sat at a booth. Beside us, the conveyor belt rolled pillowy oblongs of sushi at shoulder height. Rosa and Li sat next to each other. Closer than they needed to, I couldn't help but notice. I took one of the small white bowls, poured soy sauce over translucent leaves of ginger, a greying ball of wasabi.

Here, I showed them, using chopsticks to mix everything together. *This is what you do.*

Thank you, Li said, smiling. *I know.*

I pulled plates from the conveyor belt and set them down between us.

Don't worry, I said. *This is on me.*

I gestured for them to help themselves, feeling noble, a manager treating her team. Though paying for things on the ship didn't really mean anything after a while. Sometimes I was in the red, sometimes I wasn't. Either way, it all went back to the *WA*. I'd get nervous when I had to pay for things with cash on land, the terrible feeling of permanence. *Institutionalized*, Mia once said.

Thank you, Li repeated. *That's very kind.*

Rosa ordered a beer and Li asked for a small glass of wine. I noticed neither of them wore varnish. Their nails were naked, cut to the quick. When the drinks arrived they clinked glasses and exchanged a quietly embarrassed look. It occurred to me they were actually friends and I felt immediately threatened by this revelation. Around us, guests were being loud and vulgar. I felt the need to reassert myself. To mine for some scrap of status.

So, as your boss, I said, *I want you to know you can come to me with anything.*

Have you ever been a manager before? Rosa asked.

Have you ever worked at a nail salon before? Li added.

I've never worked at a salon, I answered. *And this is my first time managing. But that doesn't matter because I am a close personal friend of Keith's and he is very confident about my abilities as your manager.*

I stared at Rosa and Li. They were sitting so close together. A set of evil twins from a nightmare.

We didn't mean it like that, Rosa said. *We think you're doing a good job, baby.*

I busied myself with my sushi, my fingers stained with wasabi and soy sauce.

You know, in Chinese culture, Li said, *how high you hold your chopsticks is said to determine your intelligence. The higher you hold them, the smarter you allegedly are.*

I looked at my right hand, wrapped low around the chopsticks. I felt like a schoolgirl hunched over an exam.

That doesn't sound right, I said. *And anyway, these chopsticks are Japanese.*

~~~~~

I walked home via the external decks. The evening was warm and damp, curled at the edges. Fairy lights braided through the railings, twinkling off and on. Exotic insects engaged in esoteric mating rituals. The sea looked black and shiny, almost varnished. And although I felt not good about the team meal, and had decided I wouldn't do it again, I felt good in general. I found myself on the route I usually took to Keith's office and thought, maybe I should drop by? I wasn't dressed for the occasion and it was unlikely he would be in at this time, and yet I had the sure feeling of an opportunity unfurling. I suspected that he wanted me to visit, that he would be glad of the company. I continued in the direction of his executive suite, trying not to overthink it.

I paused outside reception. The lights were switched off and there was no one around. I felt like a thief, an interloper, someone knowingly breaking the rules. There was a thin line of light at the bottom of Keith's door and I walked towards it, wondering whether I should tread loudly to let him know someone was there, or quietly to surprise him. I opted for the latter, tentatively approaching. I had to knock a few times before he finally answered. I pushed open the door.

Hello? I said, stepping in. I looked down at myself, my worn *WA* tracksuit. A tracksuit was such a normal sight on the *WA*, many of the guests wore tracksuits to black tie dinners. But in front of Keith it felt slovenly and inappropriate, like I'd shown up in pyjamas, no bra.

Ingrid, Keith said. He spoke with some trepidation, like he had momentarily forgotten who I was. As I moved towards him he looked at me with a combination of curiosity and alarm.

May I? I held my palm out towards the chair.

Please do, Keith replied. *What are you doing here?*

I was in the area, I said, gesturing generally, *and I thought I would pop by*.

I sat down and wondered whether what I was doing was unusual. Perhaps it was fine, quite ordinary, to drop in unannounced. One of the many privileges of the programme. I watched Keith's face, the face of a man trying to reconcile all the different things they knew about a person. A face I had seen on my husband too many times to count. I half-wished Keith would look at me with the same bored neutrality my husband eventually did, once he had made those reconciliations. His current look made me nervous.

Well it's unusual, Keith said finally. *But you're here now. So let's have a drink.*

He reached beneath his desk to retrieve a bottle one third full of honey-coloured liquid. The sight made my mouth go dry. From a drawer he produced two heavy glasses. He opened up the bottle and poured us both a measure. I wondered what was going on.

Japanese whisky, Keith said, lifting up the glass.

I didn't know Johnnie Walker was Japanese, I replied.

I picked up the glass he had placed in front of me and cradled its weight in my palm. I thought about how it was exactly the right weight to straighten me out. I imagined an iron moving across a fabric riven with creases, the hot, smooth flat of it once it had been pressed. I longed to be able to have just enough to straighten me out. To flatten out my creases.

I can't, I said, putting it back on the desk and pushing it away. Keith put both hands flat against the polished wood and looked me dead in the eye.

Here's what's going to happen, Ingrid, he said. *You are going to have that drink and you are going to enjoy it. That's all. Do you understand?*

Sometimes when I sat with him in that small room, at the top of the ship, the space his desk occupied, the space separating us, felt insurmountable. But in that moment it dissolved to nothing.

Yes, I said. *I understand.*

Very good, he said.

I lifted the glass to my mouth, holding his gaze. I let whisky coat my lips. It tasted hot and sour, like spiced lemons, and burned my throat.

Good, he said. *Good girl.*

I drank my whisky in careful, measured sips. Keith barely touched his, just watched me from across his desk. The ship was swaying gently. I felt the air contract and expand. Through the window, the dark vinyl of the ocean, moving in undulations. I sipped again, letting the liquid sit on my tongue, heat rippling across my chest.

After a while I noticed Keith leaning over, his face close to his desk, his hand moving beneath it. He was clutching a blunt, stubbed pencil. Pushing it across expensive-looking paper. He moved his head, stared off to the side, and I saw what he was drawing. He was drawing my hand. He was drawing my hand, rested in my lap, my broken finger wrapped in gauze. I moved it nearer to him, gently lifting it on to the table to rest beside my glass, but I didn't say anything, and he carried on, looking up and then back down at the page, drawing in slow, rhythmic strokes. He stopped when I had finished my drink, watching me set the glass back on the table. He slipped the drawing into his desk drawer. Neither of us acknowledged what had happened.

You know, I've been thinking about you, he said, after a little while. *And I've got plans. For you. For all of us.*

Really? I said.

You'll see, he said.

I nodded and reached for the bottle in front of me.

No, Ingrid. Keith spoke very quietly. *One is enough.*

On the walk back to my cabin I didn't think about drinking. As I readied myself for bed I didn't think about drinking. As I lay in bed, unable to sleep, the room moving backwards and forwards, I didn't think about drinking. I didn't let myself think about anything at all.

~~~~~

The memo came a month later. An appointment to visit the hospital for what I assumed to be some kind of check-up. I'd needed to use the hospital a few times previously. For a blocked salivary gland that bloomed overnight into a semi-soft golf ball. For an isolated patch of dermatitis coating my stomach in a constellation of itchy pustules. But there had never been any follow-up. I'd just received my medication and instructions on how to dispense it and whatever complaint had gone away. Perhaps because a broken finger was a bigger deal. They wanted to make certain it wasn't interfering with my work.

In the consulting room I found the same nurse who had treated me previously, but otherwise, the room looked completely different from before. The clean white table had been replaced by a smaller, metal one, with various silver tools laid out on one side, like mismatched cutlery at a potluck. Several large cardboard boxes were stacked up on the back counter, each of them labelled *Medical Supplies*.

The nurse herself seemed different too. She had switched her tunic for a green doctor's gown. She greeted me without fully meeting my eye. I wondered if she was ill or more shy than I had remembered, or possibly just badly autistic. There was a small stool in front of the table and I sat on it, rolling up my sleeves and placing my hand in front of her. I wondered how many other jobs there were in which two people sat opposite each other across a table, while one of them tended to the other's hands.

Great, she said, looking at it. *So you know what we're here for?*

Know what? I replied.

About the procedure.

What procedure?

She looked uncertain. *You're here about the procedure on your finger, right?*

Yes, I replied. *I broke my finger. I was told to come in for a check-up. I actually removed the cast already. I hope that's OK.* She still looked impassive. *Is this not a check-up?*

Oh, she said. *Oh no.*

She released my hand and stood up, moving to retrieve something from the counter. She brought back a laminated piece of paper and laid it on the table in front of me. It had a photograph of Keith in the top right corner, and in the top left corner was the *WA*'s logo. It was a letter.

Dear Crew,

I am writing with some exciting news!

One of the founding principles of wabi sabi is that everything, and I mean everything, is coming out of and going back into nothingness. This is true of the WA. *It is true of each one of you. It is even true of me. And we cannot be our best and most authentic selves until we accept this truth.*

To demonstrate your commitment to becoming your authentic self, I am inviting you to make a special gesture of celebration. The procedure is a shared experience, a powerful act of self-determination, an embodiment of team spirit. It is also a kind of uniform, allowing you to carry the torch of the WA *wherever you go in the world. We ARE the* WA. *We are it.*

I believe in every single one of you and I love every single one of you. Please do think about that before making your decision.

Arigato,

Keith

The procedure? I said. *What is it?*

It's a gesture, the nurse replied. *It's a demonstration of your commitment.*

But what is it? I said.

It's an acknowledgement, the nurse replied. *It's a sacrifice.*

But what actually is it? I repeated, my voice high and strained, unfamiliar.

It's an amputation, she said. *We will be amputating your finger.*

I looked down at my hand. The skin around my finger was pinched and flabby where the bone had broken. My ring finger, the finger my husband had once pushed a plain gold band over, with more force than I think he had anticipated. He was taking my finger. He was taking another little piece of me.

Here, the nurse said, blankly professional. *Let me get you a glass of water.*

I shook my hands and rolled my shoulders. There seemed to be an enormous amount of adrenaline moving through my body. I had the feeling I might start laughing hysterically or get up and run straight at a wall. When the glass of water appeared in front of me I drank it all, though most of it spilled over the sides and splashed in my lap. I tried holding my breath for ten seconds, exhaled in awkward, syncopated puffs. I felt a strong urge to be inside a warm, dark room with only my own thoughts. I closed my eyes but it didn't feel sufficient and so I pressed both palms hard against my eyelids, considered lying down on the floor. I tried to make sense of things. A gesture. A commitment. An amputation. Something necessary, as most things seemed to be.

I thought about the commitments I had already made to the *WA*. I thought about my alternatives, about what it might mean not to commit. I had nothing else waiting for me. I started making a list of everybody who had ever loved or at least unequivocally liked me. Mum, Dad, my husband, Ethan, and of course, Mia and Ezra.

I thought about my husband shouting at me from the doorway, the first time I'd seen him smoke. I thought about my mum in the car, the rain against the windscreen. I thought about my dad eating dinner, winding spaghetti on to his fork. The memories felt unreal, like something I'd seen on TV. An anecdote only half-true. I thought about how it felt to be a fragment of a person moving through the world. How joining the *WA* had felt like giving my whole self over to something, the sheer relief of it, even if just for a second.

What does it involve? I asked.

We will cut off part of your finger, she said. *Around the spot where you broke it last time, by the look of things.*

She withdrew a pen from her pocket and drew a line on her own finger to demonstrate, a little above the second knuckle. I rubbed my eyes then gripped the empty glass just to feel something cool. *Do I have to say yes?* I asked.

No, she replied. *No, you don't have to. It's not mandatory.*

Will you be doing it? I asked.

She stared off to the side, to the smooth, plain walls. *I haven't had my appointment yet*, she said. She looked uncomfortable, even slightly lost. There was something about her manner that made me feel triumphant. A thought emerged in a very quiet voice. I could do this. I was strong. I had been chosen. And I had been chosen first.

Tell me about the procedure, I said.

It will be under local anaesthetic. You won't feel a thing. We will begin by sterilizing the area, then we will cut away the skin, muscular tissue, and eventually, we will cut through the bone. We will then denude the cartilage and smooth out the fracture. Finally, we stitch the skin. It will take less than an hour. She stood up and went back to the counter, returning with a tray of items I didn't want to look at. Her face was grimly determined. *I'll put up a partition and I'll also give you a set of headphones, so you won't be able to see or hear it. How does that sound?*

I'm going to stand over there, I said, pointing to the corner of the room which was furthest from the metal table. I did not feel as confident as I had a moment earlier. *I'm going to stand over there for a second and think.*

I went to the corner and turned my back to the room. I felt like that little boy in the film *The Blair Witch Project*. I heard her making various noises and tried not to determine what those noises meant. I concentrated on what I could see. The way the lip of the countertop curved out of sight. A soft browning on the pale plastic of the wall. All the while my heart was moving in my chest like a trapped animal. Your thoughts inform your feelings, I heard an old therapist tell me. No shit, I remembered thinking.

After a little while the nurse announced that she was ready. I saw she had erected a small screen, a square of thin blue material, with a vertical slit down the middle. I sat back on the stool and delivered my hand inside the blue square. I could see her eyes hovering over the screen.

She told me she would begin by administering the anaesthetic. I felt several moderately painful pinpricks followed by a rush of cool, a feeling like running water. We waited in silence for a few uncomfortable moments before she started squeezing my finger, moving along the bone. She told me she was going to prick me to make sure the anaesthetic had worked. I felt pressure but no pain. My life would have been a lot more straightforward, I thought, if I could feel only pressure but no pain. *I think it's worked*, I told her, and she blinked at me from across the table. We were ready to begin.

What would you like to listen to?

What have you got?

Um, she said. *We have Eric Clapton. We have Madonna. We have Cher. We have Al Stewart.*

Madonna, I said. *I'll go with that.*

She got up and came around the screen, lowering a large pair of heavy headphones over my head. They sat just beneath my earlobes. I saw her tap at her tablet and the music came on, loud enough that I couldn't hear anything else. Still, I gestured for her to turn up the volume and she did. I watched her wash her hands and put on gloves and a surgical mask while 'Into the Groove' played so loudly I could feel it fluttering my eyelashes. She sat back at the table. She nodded at me for confirmation. I nodded back. Her eyes fell to my hand and she went to work.

I put myself out of the room.

On the other side of the screen I could see her swollen, hooded eyelids, occasionally flicking up, her pupils contracting. And I could feel things happening. Lax, liquid things. Later, more precise motions. I just kept narrowing in on her eyes like they were a nail bed at the salon, the feathery creases at the sides and the tiny hairs at the inner corners. I had the urge to hum, starting off low, then steadily increasing in volume. I wondered whether she would find that distracting. I wondered whether she wanted to be doing what she was doing. How many people across the world were doing what they actually wanted to be doing, at that moment in time? Finally, she stood up. A spool of dark thread between her fingers, wound up like bubblegum.

All done, she said.

Did I feel a part of myself coming away? It seemed the parts of myself that came away were never really felt, only noticed once departed.

Can I look? I asked.

She removed her mask, her face beneath it grey. *Go ahead.*

I pulled my hand through the curtain and sure enough most of my finger had gone. I couldn't feel it, partly because of the anaesthetic, partly because it was no longer attached to my body. But I suspected once the anaesthetic had faded I would be able to feel it again. Feel its itches and aches. Its tingles and scratches. I knew that my nervous system and brain might take a while to catch up. Hard work, remapping those outer reaches. One less fingertip to run across soft fabric. One less fingertip to hold against my face. Oh dear, I thought.

It was flatter than I had expected and stitched with five cartoonishly grotesque stitches. I was very strong, I reminded myself. I had done something amazing. I noticed the thread was sea green, as terrible things tended to be.

I'll give you some painkillers, the nurse said. *And you will need to bathe it regularly in saline.*

OK, I said.

So we're all done, she said. She gazed at me expectantly.

I looked down at my hand, its ruptured skyline. I felt my chest tighten with many things. I would have loved a drink then. I would have loved one hundred. I am very strong, I repeated. It was proving to be a good mantra.

Are you able to share some feedback with Keith? I asked.

I am, the nurse replied.

I looked again at my hand and an emotion announced itself. Pride, I realized I was feeling. A small jolt of pride. I gathered my thoughts and then spoke. *Can you please tell Keith that it is my opinion the procedure should not be optional?*

She exhaled while checking the watch attached to her front pocket.

Sure, she replied. *I'll let him know.*

~~~~

It was just a finger, I told myself. Not even a whole finger, just a small part of it. Still, there were moments in which I felt my whole body had been disturbed, some combination of light and movement and air missing. The hand actually felt heavier without it. I kept staring at the sutured end, thinking it must be infected, bacteria running through my veins, some poison seeping through me, some reason for the way I was feeling.

I was given two days off work and I slept for most of it. Waking to drink glasses of water over the basin. To bathe my finger in warm bowls of saline. Perhaps it was the painkillers that were making me sleep, because even during my waking moments I felt only half there, forgetting things as they were happening, coming to in the bathroom and wondering how I'd found my way in there. Every time I closed my eyes I clung to the vain promise of restfulness, but I'd wake feeling exhausted, in greater need of rest than when I'd dropped off.

It was poor-quality sleep, the sort where you remain semi-aware of your surroundings, the boundary between consciousness and sleep blurring. I couldn't tell whether the images I had of myself moving around my room, moving around the ship, were memories or dreams. I'd trawl through banal scenes for telltale absurdities, instances of incoherence, to convince myself that I had been sleeping, that these things did not happen. But the perpetual sleep was also a good thing. It blanketed the unrelenting feeling of nausea and dread.

During moments of greater clarity I would message Mia and Ezra, ask them to bring things for me, granola bars or pistachio nuts or ham sandwiches from the crew mess. I couldn't let myself tell them what had happened to me, what was going to happen to them. Instead, I told them I was ill. I had come down with a fever and a bout of sickness and all of my limbs hurt, none of which was untrue. When I heard them knocking at my locked door I either remained silent or shouted for them to leave whatever they had brought me outside. We didn't need to explain these sorts of things to each other. They'd just arrange the food in a neat pile and leave. I'd wait a few minutes before retrieving it, just to be sure.

The night before I was due to go back to work, I stopped taking my painkillers. I knew I wouldn't be able to work with the precision I needed to if I was still on them. I wasn't looking forward to feeling wakeful but I was strangely not scared of the pain. There were moments when I even longed for it. I knew it was there, could sense it rolling beneath the drugs, aching to make itself known. When I was due my dose I felt a low-level soreness, the pain still diluted, which increased steadily in severity until the wound felt heavy with it.

The size of the pain, it seemed, did not correlate with the size of the wound. The pain was washing-machine or livestock sized, the wound less than one inch across. I found I could not sleep without the aid of medication. I stared up at the ceiling, feeling pain pulsing around my finger.

~~~~~

I got out of bed earlier than I would ordinarily, aware everything was going to take longer. I showered with my wounded hand hanging by my side, grateful for the practice I'd already had with that. I dried my hair and applied make-up, ate a granola bar while staring at myself in the mirror. I was going to have to explain to Rosa and Li, there was no scenario in which I could not. I mentally rehearsed how I was going to tell them. I thought about how to deliver the news sensitively, to make it seem less frightening for them. To calm them down, if need be.

When I arrived at the salon, Li was not on reception. In the back, I could hear Rosa humming while sanitizing the equipment.

Where's Li? I called.

She's gone, she replied.

Gone where?

She's gone, Rosa repeated, emerging into the main room. *She left when we docked. She got the same memo you did, baby.* She tilted her head towards my hand.

Oh, I said.

Oh, Rosa mimicked, raising her eyebrows.

I was the first, I said.

Really? She cocked her head ever so slightly. *How do you know?*

I smiled patiently at her, not wanting her to feel bad for asking such a ridiculous question. *Why did Li leave?*

Rosa went back into the sterilizing room and I followed her. She pressed open the glowing door to the sterilizer. Spaceship-blue light, an other-worldly object. She removed the recently sterilized utensils, nail files and cuticle trimmers, objects of bodily violence, folded up in a soft white cloth like a burrito. I thought about the hospital and the things that had been done to me. I had consented, I reminded myself. I had been given a choice. I was strong.

Because she wouldn't have it, Rosa shrugged. *She's young. She has options. Why should she?*

But you're going to have it?

Next week, baby. Chop, chop.

She lifted up her left hand and made a scissoring motion with her right. I tried to read the expression on her face, somewhere between sincere and crazy. There was something unsinkable about her, I realized. She reminded me of Mia. I supposed that was why I liked her.

She paced through to the main room and began laying out the equipment.

I have a lot of debt, she said, mainly to herself. I remembered her telling me that before she joined the *WA* she had worked in hospitality and sales. She used her savings to invest in various businesses. A wedding-planning website. A location-scouting company. A farm-to-table restaurant. She'd had a lot of bad luck. She'd also told me she had a son.

You can't actually feel anything, I offered. *It's all under anaesthetic. And you get to choose a song.*

Really?
Really.
We should open up, she said.

I straightened my shoulders. *We should open up,* I told her.

I went to unlock the door, kicked a stopper underneath it. I looked around at the salon, bright and inviting, somewhere you'd come to get clean. I gave the polishes within reach a quick shake, took a look at the bookings. Rosa positioned herself on one of the bamboo chairs, smoothed out her tunic and practised a smile. She spread her fingers out on the table, nails unpainted but immaculately clean.

What song are you going to choose? I asked.

I don't know, she replied, idly. *Maybe Prince.*

~~~~~

In the days that followed, I continued to feel conflicted about the procedure. Pain flickered electronically up and down my arm, making working on manicures that much harder. I'd never had a complicated relationship with my body, it was basically functional. It felt balanced and easy to move in. But now one side had been chipped away and the whole thing had been thrown off. I became preoccupied with the thought of the amputated fingers. Where did they go? Where were they being kept? Though the more time that passed, the more I came to understand the procedure's necessity.

When I held a customer's fingers they no longer latticed like an expensive pie crust, instead making a more avant-garde shape, like a Mondrian painting. I found myself admiring the vacant space, this recently occupied blank. The implicit tentativeness of my body as a whole. The perfection of imperfection. The attentiveness impermanence required. My body was a thing moving out of and into nothingness. How could I have forgotten?

From then, I kept an eye on the shedding parts of myself. The knotted clumps of hair in the corners of my cabin. The curl of a toenail come loose from a toe. They were reminders, tokens, talismans. They were everywhere. I felt awake, really wide awake, for the first time in a long time. Keith had awakened us.

It was fortunate I was feeling awake as I had very little time to sleep. Rosa and I were now the only people working at the salon and we had a steady stream of guests who wanted their bodies pampered and prettified. So many hands to soak in warm water. So many feet to coat in oil. While I went to work on guests' nails I would ask them how they were enjoying their stay, how long they had been away. They would tell me about the meals they had eaten and the trinkets they had bought and the activities they had participated in and the relative plushness of their cabins. They would never ask about my finger, though I could tell they had noticed.

We ate what we could along the way. Crescent moons of mango, pots of yoghurt and honey, slices of rye bread spread with cream cheese. We drank bottles of coconut water and pineapple juice, pulling them from the mini-fridge where they chilled beside congealing bottles of varnish. Once we had closed for the day, Rosa would wordlessly clean the salon, pushing a felt cloth over smooth surfaces, scrubbing the rusting corners of metal, while I went over the accounts. I reviewed the bookings we had for the following day and put together a rota that would allow us time for separate trips to the toilet. I audited our equipment and supplies and reordered any items we might need delivering the next time we docked.

In the evenings I threw myself into the programme. Keith had given me extensive reading materials on wabi sabi, mostly written by himself. I annotated them then emailed over short essays surmising my thoughts. A number of new management tutorials had been released and I downloaded them all. Direction and Leadership. Conflict Management and Resolution. Coaching and Mentoring. Advanced Assertiveness Skills.

Most days I woke early and headed to the salon, arrived back in my cabin armed with plastic boxes of food, then worked until I went to sleep. There was something nulling about the experience. The small number of options I'd become accustomed to had been scrubbed clean. But I didn't mind running out of options. Whenever one excused itself I felt only cool, certain relief. I felt virtuous, at once empty and full. I felt a purity akin to starvation.

~~~~~

Ezra, Mia and I had not seen each other for a few weeks, the longest since we'd first met. They would still message on our shared thread, trying to work out a time to meet. We tried to make our time off align, like turning the segments of a Rubik's cube, hoping for a miracle. Often, I would neglect to respond to these conversations until days later. Occasionally I would forget altogether. Though sometimes at night I would wake to a terrible, amorphous feeling, hot and oppressive. I would hold my breath and blink in the dark, wondering what it was. And then I would realize, it was just them. I just wanted to see them.

I often dreamt about them too. I would dream I was alone in an empty apartment in the middle of a big city, a large meal prepared and a place set for Mia. I would dream I was on a flight with a seat left vacant beside me. Ezra's seat. In these dreams I would wait, and when I woke up I would keep waiting, lying very still in my bed, letting my waking life flush out my dream one, though the longing still remained. But then the disappointment would settle, the room would come back into focus.

Eventually we found a time when we were all free. I had an afternoon off, a pocket of a few hours. We arranged to meet in the atrium, surrounded by velvet and gold. I was the last to arrive, finding them sat down, their backs straight and their lounge chairs pulled close together, speaking in serious tones. A few feet away, a pianist played jazz standards. They both turned their heads when they saw me walking over but neither of them said hello.

Are you hungry? Ezra quickly broke the silence.

I'm OK, I said. *I ate on the way here.*

We ordered some croquettes, he said. *Would you like a croquette?*

Mia pulled back her chair to make space for me and I pulled over a squat little stool, moved myself between them. Mia's body was arched defensively. She looked like she was deep in conversation with herself and various emotions passed across her face.

Mia, I said reluctantly. *Is everything OK?*

Everything's fine, she said. She pushed her fingers into the plump seams of the seat.

Is it? I said, perhaps more aggressively than I had intended.

Not really, she replied, after a moment of silence. *No.*

She removed her hand from where it was tucked. It took me a second or two to understand what she was showing me, so accustomed had I become to my own hand. I felt a much deeper sense of loss looking at Mia's. I'd always liked her hands. They were so small and precise. Her skin was very soft, almost poreless. It seemed a more extreme violence, to cut a piece of them away.

I felt a sickness low in my stomach as I turned to look at Ezra, who placed his hand on his knee, wordlessly contemplating the trauma. His finger was much redder. Still fresh and less neatly finished, like it had been torn out from the joint. It reminded me of an afternoon long before the *WA*, baking an elaborate cake for my husband, finally dropping it on the floor. Surrounded by sponge, fruit and frosting, crying against the oven. Another thing I had ruined. I held my breath. I would not allow myself to cry.

You didn't think to tell us? Mia said, her voice steady and controlled.

I thought about the many times I had pictured myself telling them. Rearranging the words I would use, hoping for the perfect fit. I'd made a choice in not choosing, I knew that.

Aren't you going to say anything? Did you know about this?

I moved my stool so it was opposite Mia. I remembered my

Conflict Management and Resolution tutorial. A graph which measured optimal performance against stress severity and duration. How stress suppresses the brain's ability to produce new cells. How you can manage stress by managing all the different parts of your body. You can measure your breathing. You can keep your arms and legs perfectly still. I took a deep breath, gathered my hands in my lap.

Everything, I said, very calmly, *is coming out of and going into nothingness.*

What?

Everything, I repeated, *is coming out of and going into nothingness. Including you. Including Ezra. Including me.* I met her eyes and counted to five, relaxing my shoulders.

What the fuck? Mia said, louder than before, though she could see I was right in front of her. I could hear her perfectly well.

It takes a while, I offered. *But you will start to understand soon.*

I tried to imagine my movements like slow, certain waves. I looked at Mia and Ezra in turn, the muscles of my face immobile. I got up without saying another word, rising into the easy cool of the atrium and breathing fully, at last.

~~~~~

I was due to see Keith again. I wore Mia's dress, which was starting, more noticeably, to smell. I fished a slice of lemon from an empty glass of soda water, removed the stringy flesh, and ran the rind around the collar of the dress. It reminded me of a time in my late teens, when my parents let me spend a weekend with a friend. A rare concession after thoroughly vetting her parents. We took ourselves to a music festival, sleeping outside in a tent, drinking and speaking to strangers. Things which would have rendered my parents apoplectic had they known. I bought myself a T-shirt from a hippy stand and wore it for the entire festival, and then too the whole week after, so attached was I to the physical remnants of that weekend. I didn't wash it until my mother literally tore it from my hands and after that it was never the same.

I decided to take a little walk ahead of my meeting. I wanted to see the sun and the sea, to breathe the salt air. I strolled along one of the upper decks. Though it was quite early there were a few people up and about. Couples nibbling on pretzels, old people playing shuffleboard. I walked past a man licking foam from his coffee, moving in the opposite direction. I passed a large family holding cups of shaved ice, brightly coloured and luminous, like semi-precious stones. It felt good, I thought, to wake up and eat. I felt something happening to my brain, a piece of un-tender meat pulverized into softness. My face was misted with sea air, my lungs felt disinfected.

I reached the end of the walkway and followed the staircase down to the deck below. It was a lot busier than the one above, partly because it had a swimming pool, albeit a small one, kidney-shaped, with a single inflatable flamingo marooned in the middle. Around it, people were already sunbathing on loungers and the air smelled strongly of sunscreen.

There was a bar to the side of the pool which sold ice lollies and pisco sours. Across the bar top were empty glasses, the remains of the previous night, so many that a couple had evidently toppled over the side, smashing on the polished wooden deck. I looked back to the pool and noticed empty glasses set on the floor beside the sunloungers too, plus the occasional paper napkin gone astray. My plimsolls crunched on a patch of broken glass. I wondered whether I had a responsibility here, to step in and sweep up. Instead I retreated in the direction of Keith's office, the comforting familiarity of the receptionist's indifference, the pleasingly straight-backed seats.

In the waiting room I sat in my usual spot. There were only two other members of the programme waiting. No Kai. No man with the mole. I supposed the others had dropped out. I looked down at my hand. It was no longer surprising. After a little while Keith appeared in the doorway and beckoned me in.

Ingrid, he said. *It's good to see you again. And the famous dress.*

Thank you, I replied.

I could smell the wood of the furniture, feel the heat from the tea on his desk. I felt like a deer in the forest, alert to every rustle or snapped twig. I imagined Keith low in the grass, tenderly cradling a rifle. *What are we going to talk about today, I wonder?* He gazed at me intently.

I smiled back. I wondered whether I should bring up the procedure. Instead, I decided to wait until he brought it up. To allow him to take the lead.

Is there anything you would like to ask me about? Keith prompted.

No, I said. *Nothing comes to mind.*

Interesting, he replied. *Are you sure?* He lifted his hand from his lap and placed it on the desk. *You wouldn't like to talk about this?*

I regarded his amputated finger. On seeing Mia's and Ezra's hands, I was struck by the violence. Torn sinew and sliced-open skin. But on him, the finger, or half-finger, looked a little amusing. There was nothing brutal about it. It seemed sweet, somehow. A holiday trinket to be dangled from a keychain. A small sausage, burst in the pan.

I was the first to have it done, he said. *Lead by example.*

Oh. I felt, just momentarily, a murderous rage.

He stretched his fingers out in front of him, holding them up against the light. The sun splintered through them.

I think it looks good, I said, recovering myself.

It does, he replied.

I looked around the room and thought about men and their offices. I used to visit my husband in his office. I'd surprise him with a salad or a home-made piece of quiche. Later in the evening I'd go to throw something in the bin and discover my offerings, wilted lettuce and curdled pieces of egg. I'd ask him whether he had enjoyed his lunch and he would tell me, *Delicious!*

My husband had an office a bit like this, I said.

I'm sure he did not, Keith replied.

I looked at my hand again. A symbol of strength.

Did you get my message? I asked.

Which message?

About the procedure, I said. *The nurse said it was optional, but I told her that wasn't right. I asked her to pass the message on to you.*

No. He was sitting completely still, impassive. *No message.*

Are you sure?

Of course I'm sure, Ingrid, he replied.

It felt like there was some discrepancy of perspective which increased the longer we looked at each other. A reverse zoom.

My friends are upset with me, I said. *They're upset about the procedure.*

I'm not surprised. They don't get it.

But they had it done. They chose it.

Friendships are imperfect, Keith said. *And they are impermanent. They are not supposed to last because nothing is. Do you really need me to tell you that?*

No, I replied, chastened. *I understand.*

I could see he was frustrated. He lifted up his tablet, also cracked, I noticed, and made exaggerated swiping gestures against the glass. I wondered whether it ever cut his fingers, as it occasionally did mine.

Shall we get started, he said. *We don't have all day.*

I nodded meekly.

OK, he said. *So maybe let's talk about friendship. Such a flawed thing at the best of times. Can you recall a memory about a bad friendship?*

I looked around the room while I thought, resting my eyes on various objects. More were broken than the last time I had visited. A shattered picture frame. A lampshade torn in two. I almost forgot why I was there, so reassuring was it, looking at the damaged decorations. But then I remembered the friend I had gone to the music festival with. Her name was Anna.

I've got one, I said, triumphant.

Go ahead, Keith nodded.

When I was a teenager I had a friend called Anna, I said. *She came over one Friday evening. My parents ordered us a pizza and rented us a film. They let us sit in the living room. It was a real treat. After the film had finished, we watched some TV. A programme about a charity for abandoned dogs. When it finished, my mum walked into the living room, turned off the TV and said,* Bed. *Just like that. I stood up from the sofa and told Anna it was time for bed. We slept top to tail. Lying in the dark, she asked me if I always went to bed when my mum told me to. I told her I did. Why wouldn't I?*

I fell silent and waited for Keith to say his part. Eventually he opened his eyes and asked, *And then?*

That's it, I replied. *We went to sleep. Now shall I do it again?*

Keith looked irritated. *Again*, he said. *Tell me again.*

I had a friend called Anna, I repeated. *My parents would not usually let me have friends over, but they would let me have Anna because they said she came from a good family. She came round one Friday evening. We must have been seventeen. They ordered us a pizza and rented us a film. They let us sit in the living room. Dad was sorting things out in the garden. Mum was making something in the kitchen. They left us alone.*

After the film had finished, we asked if we could watch some TV. They said we could so long as they picked the programme. They chose one about a charity for abandoned dogs. When it finished, my mum walked into the living room, turned off the TV and flatly stated, Bed. *I stood up from the sofa, tidied up the cushions, and told Anna again, because she hadn't seemed to hear.* Come on, *I said.* We have to go to bed. *She followed me up the stairs and we slept top to tail. Lying in the dark, she asked me if I always went to bed when my mum said,* Bed. *And I told her I did. There was no point lying. She could see how it was.*

Keith's forehead was creased, his jaw firmly set. He regarded me suspiciously, moved his head to one side. *What's going on?* he said, after a long pause.

What do you mean? I felt suddenly panicked.

Are you deliberately trying to sabotage what we're doing here? Do you

have so much ego that you can't submit to this process for a few minutes?
Do you really think that highly of yourself?

I tried to respond but I had the feeling I might cry. I bit the tip of my tongue until it passed, dug my remaining fingernails into my hand. Keith stared back at me from across the table, suddenly indifferent, almost bored. Behind him, the sea was moving in slow waves, the sun white and round above it. It occurred to me that I had no idea how to read Keith, the many things he contained. He was as vast and opaque as the ocean. I worried about how much longer I might stay interesting to him. My legs felt heavy. My dress smelled sour.

Keith picked up his tablet. *I think we should leave it for today*, he announced.

I'm sorry, I said. *I have a lot on my mind.*

I still believe in you, he replied, already absorbed by his screen. *Despite what has happened today. I still believe you can be your best self.* He glanced up briefly. *You haven't forgotten what I told you?*

I shook my head and stood up, pushing down the curled hem of my dress. He didn't watch me leave.

～～～

Outside Keith's office I felt cast off, jettisoned. I had a strong urge to be reabsorbed by the *WA*, to be at the heart of it, surrounded by expensively dressed strangers, spectacle and nothingness. I made my way back to the deck with the kidney pool, finding it in further disarray. There were many more passengers out, shorts rolled up, cooling their legs in the milky pool water. The pink flamingo was almost entirely deflated, crumpled on the water's surface like a skin. The pool smelled chalky and over-chlorinated. The passengers themselves were notably unglamorous. They seemed, to various degrees, to have given up. Their clothes were creased and stained. Their hair was unclean, or over-bleached, and splitting in the sun.

I removed my heels and sat down alongside the dishevelled

passengers, dipping my bare legs into the water. I lay back and let out a loud, lengthy sigh, something between the start of a conversation and a cry. I focused all my frustration into my hand, balling my four and a half digits into a fist. I slammed it once to the floor, so hard I grazed the skin from the soft underside. I allowed myself one more sigh, this one closer to a scream, then I got up to put my shoes back on. I walked to my cabin without looking back at the pool, knowing I had not inconvenienced anyone, no one was troubled by what I had done. No one had noticed at all.

Back in my manicurist uniform, in the spa-like setting of the salon, I started to feel calm. The glass bottles of nail varnish were cool in my hand. I had a full afternoon of working on the soft planes of strangers' fingernails. I interacted with Rosa minimally. I felt grateful for the light sounds of my work. The delicate chimes of metal touching glass. Once our last customers had left, Rosa and I silently went about our clean-up, and then we left together but without either of us saying goodbye.

~~~~~

I hadn't wanted to see Ezra and Mia. I was planning to coolly ignore their messages, leave them hanging for a little while. I was even contemplating a scenario in which I was done with them for good. But when Ezra eventually messaged I found myself replying automatically, later remembering I was supposed to be avoiding him. We talked and agreed to meet at Mia's later that week to play Families.

Mia's cabin was made up of two sets of bunk beds with a thin channel of blue carpet in-between. Damp towels and pyjama bottoms hung from the sides of the top bunks. The floor was littered with tubes of lipstick and flat circles of cotton wool. Mia's was a bottom bunk, her small allocation of wall decorated with postcards, art deco prints and pictures of rocks in the sea.

I found them sitting opposite each other on the narrow strip of floor, and I joined them, making their line into a circle, my back to the door. No one mentioned the argument. Instead, we went straight into discussing the concept for our game.

It had been a while since the last time but none of us had forgotten our place. It was Ezra's turn to be Mum, mine to be Dad, Mia's to be Baby. We decided on a scenario in which the mum was tired from spending nights in the office and the dad was struggling to pick up the slack. They had been talking about redecorating the living room since moving in three years ago but had never got around to it. Meanwhile the baby had recently moved on to solid foods and was still getting accustomed to chewing. I chopped up pieces of apricot and banana while Ezra wrapped a jumper around Mia's neck and played at cleaning up her face. I offered the plate to Mia and she clumsily mashed a piece of banana into her palm then licked bits of it from her hand.

*I can't do thi*s, she said, after a minute or two. *I can't do this if you're going to be mad with me.*

I'm not mad with you, I said. *Are you mad with me?*

I'm not, she said, and then more decisively, *I'm not.*

OK, then. I nodded. *Let's carry on, shall we?*

Mia resumed licking her hand. I asked Ezra what he thought about a warm orange or terracotta, while half-keeping an eye on her.

I'm not sure about orange, Ezra replied. *It could look garish and cheap.*

He folded a pile of Mia's clothes into small, soft squares and set them aside. He fussed with her hair, smoothing its sleek, blunt edges.

Well what about something darker? I said. *Perhaps a deep green or navy blue?*

I don't want anything too dark, Ezra said. *How about a more neutral colour? A nice biscuit tone?*

Beige, I said. *Beige is boring.*

What about a pale pink? Or mint green?

I held a cube of apricot up to Mia's mouth and she bit at it using only her lips. I watched as she sucked it, dribbling a little. I snatched one of the squares of clothing Ezra had folded to dab at her mouth.

Hey, Ezra said. *I've only just washed that.*

Well she's making a mess, I said. *Aren't you, sweetheart? You're making a mess, aren't you, little one?*

I put on a high and lilting voice when I spoke. I pinched Mia's cheek between my finger and thumb and felt an authentic swell of fear and love rising in my chest. I half-wished she really was as small as a baby, Ezra too, so I could keep them safe and with me all the time.

How about a feature wall? Ezra asked.

I fed another piece of apricot into Mia's mouth. It popped straight back out and I retrieved it from her lap, allowing her to eat it from my hand. She moved it around her open-hanging mouth, then swallowed. *We could have wallpaper for a feature wall? Something a little . . . lively?*

Mia started making upset sounds and so I gave her more banana. She munched on it happily, making slightly less of a mess.

I'm not sure about wallpaper, Ezra said. *Now you're complicating things.*

I went to feed Mia another piece of banana when I noticed her looking faintly blue. She started coughing and pawing at her throat.

She's choking, I said. *She's choking on her fruit.*

Ezra moved me out of the way, more roughly than was necessary. *Are you choking, darling?* he said.

Hit her back, I advised. *Hit her on the back.*

Mia dribbled out a piece of banana, her face reddening quickly. Even the whites of her eyes were looking rosy. She started clutching her neck, looking wild and confused, her head searching the room. Ezra struck her once, gently, on the back.

Harder, I said. *You need to hit her harder than that.*

He tapped her again, only a little harder, but Mia was still holding her breath, and now Ezra looked tearful, hitting her again and again. I was starting to get bored. *Move*, I said. *Move!*

I wrapped my legs around her, made my hands into a single fist, placed them just beneath her ribcage, and thrust them towards me. A piece of apricot flew from Mia's mouth, landing on the cotton sheet, the spot Ezra had been folding. Mia gasped for air, rolling across the floor, coughing then laughing.

I made myself choke, she wheezed. *I made myself actually choke. I made myself actually choke!*

My skin felt cold. *What?*

I wasn't faking, she said, still coughing. *I actually made myself choke. I could have died!*

She lay on her back, stretching out all her limbs. *Amazing!* she said, beatific.

Ezra crawled towards her, his face slick with tears. He pulled Mia's head on to his lap, sobbing loudly. *My baby*, he said, rocking her back and forth, dripping tears on to her face. *My poor baby.*

I stood up and watched them on the floor. Ezra's face was pale and wet. Mia's was pink and mottled. My own face spasmed with disgust.

I'm leaving, I said. Neither of them acknowledged me. *I said I'm leaving*, I repeated.

Ezra continued moving hair from Mia's face, still rocking her and crying. Mia looked up at me, her eyes pinched and bloodshot.

Please don't go, she said. *I'm sorry. I want to hear about how you're doing.*

I'm fine, I said.

The salon? she said.

The salon is good.

And the programme? It's all going well with the programme?

I thought about how I had felt during my last meeting with Keith. Like I had been shut out of a safe space, with nowhere else to go.

It's going fine, I said. *Nothing to report.*

Are you sure? Mia sounded disappointed. I studied the worried vault of her brow. I wondered whether her concern was authentic. Whether it was laced with pity or condescension.

I'm sure, I said. *Why would it not be?*

OK. We're proud of you.

I let myself out, pausing in the corridor. Their voices still murmuring from inside the room. I pretended not to hear my name.

~~~~~

Back in my cabin, I pulled the blind over my porthole. I wanted to be obliterated by darkness. My stomach rumbled and I let it. Hunger was just a sensation, I thought. A temporary state. I may have slept, waking in a light sweat as a message arrived on my tablet. I'd been given an extra day of Land Leave at short notice. I would disembark tomorrow.

I placed the tablet back on the floor and thought about whether Land Leave was something I wanted. I pressed my hand to my lower stomach, the site of my various wants. I thought back to my old flat, my life with my husband, how consumed I was by need. How it was the only thing keeping me going. How the getting never really felt as good as the wanting, but the not-getting felt fucking catastrophic. I must be better, I thought. I must be good. I mentally repeated the refrain. I must be better. I must be good. Voices from my past life periodically interrupted but I drowned them out, thinking in a louder, more urgent voice. I must be my best self. Best self. Best self. Eventually, I fell asleep. When I woke my pyjamas were sodden.

Land

The morning was warm but the breeze was surprisingly cool, giving the air a feverish feel. There was a strong smell of fish and the smell reminded me of virtually everywhere I had been. I pressed the heel of my palm to my forehead, already slick with sweat, wiping my hand against my tracksuit and walking forward. Ahead of me were two large concrete buildings with a narrow path running between them. I had the feeling that if I could withstand the grey claustrophobia of the alley I'd be rewarded with something significant at the end.

I walked down it, feeling cold and alone, until it opened up on to a car park lined with gazebos and plastic tables, all piled with second-hand clothes, fruit and vegetables, vintage postcards and other pointless objects. I looked down at my sweat-stained tracksuit and trainers. Approaching the first table, I began indiscriminately plucking items from it before remembering myself. I wanted to be a person who moved with precision, who was driven by pragmatism and logic. A person with smooth, seamless edges. I would select my outfit carefully, taking into account the weather, how I might spend my day and the colour palette of the people around me.

The seller weighed my purchases, using what appeared to be a laundry basket balanced on a set of kitchen scales, before putting them in a plastic bag. I paid, gathered up my haul, then looked around the car park for further direction. There were young families moving slowly between the stalls. Women held up pieces of fruit, squeezing to confirm their ripeness. Everyone seemed very involved. My instincts told me to find breakfast. I'd made a promise to myself not to drink until at least noon. But I still needed to eat and that gave me the beginning of a framework for my day.

I looped back to the long, wide road that ran the length of the coast. The coastline was dotted with palm trees, fanged with inscrutable modern buildings. I wondered about the significance of a building shaped like a wave, a building like a length of Toblerone. It was becoming a hot, bright day, and the road was so busy with traffic that it felt like I was walking along the precipice of a canyon. I ducked inside a public toilet to change, stacking my new clothes on top of the closed toilet. Plain white T-shirt. Tomato-red sweatshirt. Jeans covered in zipped pockets. Pair of blue sneakers. Canvas bag printed with cartoon strawberries. The jeans wouldn't quite button up so I had to pull the sweatshirt over them but overall I was pleased with the effect.

Back outside I'd had enough of the coastal road. I slipped down a small side street, passing a hardware shop, a Chinese supermarket, a second-hand bookstore, a twenty-four-hour pharmacy. I was finding land more depersonalizing than usual. Everyone seemed both real and unreal, like I had already seen them on TV. A man holding a blue-and-white-striped bag. A woman wearing nurse's scrubs. I tried to imagine the threads of their lives, how much ground they must cover in even a single day. The thought was exhausting. My own life was as small as a small backpack, sparsely filled and taken everywhere with me.

I tried to walk as close to the shopfronts as possible, leaning away from people as they passed. An estate agent's. A bakery. A shop specializing in maple syrup. I stopped to wallow in the butterscotch smell, admiring the neat rows of merchandise in the window. Maple-syrup candies, maple-syrup butter. Popcorn coated in maple syrup. There were even small beige teddy bears wearing T-shirts printed with maple leaves. The sight was bizarre until I remembered I was in Canada.

I paused outside a couple of diners, looking at the menus. Everywhere did essentially the same two things, eggs and pancakes. I chose the biggest, busiest one, somewhere I could sit and be anonymous.

Inside, a waitress took me to a high communal table and handed me a menu, running a thumb over a smear of ketchup congealed at the corner. I briefly contemplated pressing my tongue to taste it. The waitress left but came back almost immediately and I asked for eggs and tea. *Hot*, I said. *Very hot tea*. When it arrived I laced my fingers around the cup. I thought about the way heat softens muscle. Perhaps this small, hot cup would soften mine. I'd just about convinced myself it was doing the trick when a woman passed behind me, accidentally grazing me with her elbow, and I nearly jumped out of my skin. I want a drink, I thought. Wine. Beer. Dry Martini. I would have taken anything.

The eggs soon followed and I pushed them around with my fork, custard yellow, plump and fluffy. I ground sea salt and black pepper on them, cut off a triangle to bite. Rum, I thought. A rum cocktail with a tiny umbrella. Yes. No.

Along the bench from me was a man in office attire with bright red cheeks. He removed a newspaper from the leather satchel he wore across his chest and spread it out on the table. It kept touching the side of my arm, tickling me not unpleasantly. I looked sideways at him, a man in a suit reading a broadsheet newspaper. There was once a time when finding a man who wore suits, who read broadsheet newspapers, was my main motivation in life. I knew what dresses to wear, which bars to hang around at. I knew the things to say, the things not to say. It was something I got good at. I'd give my friends tips and they'd listen to me, rapt. How smug I was in my success when I introduced them to my future husband, my hand resting on his elbow. I began answering questions in the first person plural. *We're busy this weekend. We're watching this series. We're cooking a lot of Mexican food, recently!* When I joined the *WA* I had to retrain myself to respond in the singular, though even then I would occasionally slip up.

I glanced over at him again. None of the headlines in his newspaper even vaguely made sense and I didn't try to piece them together. Instead, I tucked my hair behind my ear and looked at my reflection in the window. I relaxed my face and softened my expression consciously, like I used to do before speaking to men. I took a sip of tea then angled my body towards him.

What have you got coming? I asked.

I'm sorry, he said. He seemed annoyed. *I have no idea what you're asking me.*

I mean, are you having something special? I attempted a laugh. *Pancakes? Bacon?*

I'm having a protein bowl, he said, not looking up from his newspaper. I thought about playfully pushing it aside, saying something kittenish. *Read me!*

What's a protein bowl? I wondered aloud. I remembered men in suits like it when you deferred to their knowledge of the world.

What do you think it is? he said. *It's a bowl consisting of breakfast items that are high in protein.*

The waitress walked up from behind, extending her long, slim arm between us. She placed a shallow bowl filled with crispy bacon, sliced avocado, sweet potato and black beans on the table. The man turned around as she left, looking her all the way up and down.

See, he said, turning back and pointing to his food.

He removed his knife and fork, stabbed a blackened slice of bacon.

Is it good? I asked.

Mm hmm, he said, chewing.

I looked at my reflection in the window again. I wasn't wearing any make-up. My eyes looked ill-defined and I had more pronounced nasolabial folds than the last time I had properly inspected myself. The man scooped up some beans, chewed on them while staring ahead. I lifted my chin and gathered my pride.

I am here for one day only, I said. *And if you were to meet me here, at eleven p.m. this evening, we could go back to your place, and we could do anything.*

He bit a piece of potato. Dabbed the corner of his mouth with a paper napkin.

Do you see what I am saying? I added.

You don't need to say p.m. and this evening, the man replied, gesturing with his fork. *You just need to say one or the other.*

I lowered my head, looked up at him from beneath my eyelashes. Did I seem sultry? I no longer knew. *Do you see what I am saying?* I repeated, with a graver tone.

Yeah yeah, eleven p.m., he said. *Eleven p.m. this evening. Maybe I'll be here.*

I placed my knife and fork together and left the diner without looking back, crossing the window where the man was sitting, wondering whether he would bother to check me out. Wondering whether I looked any better out in the light.

I continued walking around aimlessly. I thought about how much easier everything would be if I could have a drink. Alcohol helped me access my intuitions. It scraped out my impulses. It made a road feel like a ribbon, a day feel like an event. I made a mental list of the sorts of things people do. They go to cafes and eat croissants. They make egg and cress sandwiches and go for a hike. They sit in a Jacuzzi and talk about the news. When I ran out of ideas I walked into the first bar I saw.

It was a little decadent for my tastes. Fairy lights dangled overhead, among them a disco ball hanging static. There was a stag's head mounted on the wall, banker's lamps dotted across the long, high tables. It was a bar where everything was expensive, even a Coke, served in a glass shaped like a bird bath and finished with a twist of lime. It was strong and syrupy. It almost did the trick.

I took it over to a table nearest the window, where passers-by were walking past, holding me accountable. I sipped it watching them, mentally cataloguing the colours they were wearing. Powder pink. Canary yellow. Baby blue. I was so overwhelmed by the relentless deluge of colour that for a second I didn't notice Ezra, in denim overalls and a pale cream shirt, his face obscured by a baseball cap pulled low.

The image of him lingered for a few moments before I acknowledged it. I left my drink half-finished and ran outside. He turned around when I called his name and I ran towards him, wrapped my arms around his waist. When I pulled back he seemed mildly horrified to see me but was trying very hard to pretend otherwise. He held up a brown paper bag. *I've been shopping.*

Shopping? I echoed. I was so relieved to see him. The previous night felt reassuringly distant.

Yes, he said. *Shopping.*

What did you buy?

Plates. Plus some sort of healing crystal.

Why did you buy plates?

I don't know, he replied, swinging the bag. *They were on offer.*

I wrapped my arms around his middle again and he rested his chin on top of my head. It was the first time we had ever been on land together. I thought about Mia, about what she'd think if she could see us. I took Ezra's hand and led him back towards the bar.

Come on, I said. *Let's get a drink.*

Inside I ordered another Coke and Ezra ordered a glass of milk. If the bartender found this peculiar, he did not let on. He presented Ezra with his drink in a tall glass filled with ice, finished with a matte black swizzler. Ezra lifted it from the bar and gave it a swirl as if this was exactly what he had expected. We found a booth, sat across from each other.

It's nice, Ezra said, looking around.

It's OK, I said. *It's strange seeing you here. It feels almost forbidden.*

But it's not, Ezra replied. *Right?*

I think we're allowed. I sipped my Coke. It was starting to hurt my teeth. I wondered whether I should order a proper drink. I could have just one and no more. It was nearing midday. *Have you had much leave this year?*

A couple of days. Portugal. Guatemala. You?

Spain, I said. *And here.*

I fidgeted with the top of my jeans, sucking in my stomach, tried to pull the button towards the buttonhole. The more I struggled to make them fasten the more agitated I felt. I wanted to ask Ezra about Mia, about what she said after I left. What they had said together about me. What they thought of me. Ezra was preoccupied with the tabletop, studying the grain of the wood. I thought about drinking again. About having just one drink. I'd order just one drink, it would straighten me out, and then I'd get on with my day.

I'm going back to the bar, I said. *Do you want anything?*

Ezra lifted his empty glass. *One more*, he said.

I came back with a glass of milk for Ezra and a whisky cocktail for me. I moved the ice against the glass, took a long, slow sip. I felt it on the underside of my forearms, down the sides of my ribs. It felt like the tide slowly crawling in. I started to relax.

It's early, Ezra said. He smiled hesitantly.

This is what I do on land, I said. *I just go drinking.*

That doesn't seem like you.

It's true. I shrugged. *I usually just drink myself into oblivion.*

Ezra stared at me softly, metabolizing what I'd said. It was comforting to be seen like that. It made me feel safe for the first time in a long while. Ezra was the kind of person who took people for exactly who they were. He never wanted anything more from you than that.

Mia's lucky to have you, I said.

Are you kidding? Ezra replied. I didn't know what that meant.

I imagined them as children, then as teenagers, then as adults. I remembered Mia telling me she used to have two small dogs. That when she joined the *WA* she dropped them off at her parents'. They were biologists and they'd know what to do.

How did your parents meet? I asked him.

I dunno, he said. *Doing science? What about you?*

Um. I think a friend set them up. I didn't want to talk about my parents and regretted introducing the topic. *I'll get us something else*, I said.

Should I have a drink? He looked a little shy. *I mean, a drink like yours?*

Absolutely, I said. *That's what I'll get.*

At the bar I ordered two more whisky cocktails plus two shots of vermouth. *That your baby brother?* the bartender asked as he poured out the shots.

Sort of, I replied.

Back in the booth we sipped our cocktails, chased them with vermouth. I returned to the bar and got us two cold beers. Ezra seemed more comfortable drinking beer. He seemed more comfortable, generally. His features were less fixed, softly mutable, like a piece of clay. Everything about him seemed fluid, relaxed in a way I had never previously witnessed. Ezra always had a placid energy but usually it came from a place of naivety. A child told they will be having two birthdays and Christmases, not comprehending the broader implications of their parents' marriage collapsing. But this was different. He moved like there was nothing pushing against him.

Did you decide to join the WA *or did Mia?* I asked.

Mia, Ezra replied, foam ringing his mouth. *I had a girlfriend. I was working at a school. But I couldn't let her go on her own.*

Why?

Why? He momentarily wrinkled his forehead before lapsing back into softness. *Why do you think?*

He moved his hand across his neck, his eyelids only half-open. I needed to ask him where I stood with Mia, but he got up and went to the bathroom before I had the chance. I watched him cross the room, stumbling a little but finding his feet.

When he came back I suggested we stretch our legs, go see something. Maybe do some more shopping. Ezra seemed to like that idea. He wanted to buy a candle and so we made that the purpose of our day.

We visited a lot of shops. Enormous department stores and small independent lifestyle shops. Sniffed large pillar candles and multicoloured tea lights, occasionally licking the wax, confirming they tasted not like basil or spiced rum or freshly laundered linen, but like wax. We called into various bars on the way, sometimes sipping pale ales over plastic baskets of junk food, other times knocking back neon shots up at the bar.

The shopping made me nostalgic for my time at the gift shop. I'd always loved shops. The orderliness and certain simplicity. My first job was in a shop, a clothes shop, my last year of school. I would finish a shift and head home, finding my parents in the living room, waiting for me with the television on mute. *How was it?* they would ask. *Did you speak to anyone? Did anyone ask you your name? Did anyone try to follow you home?*

I loved that job. I loved the feeling of competence. Walking around the arid shop floor, reams of fabric flung over my elbow, saying *I'll just see if we have that in the stockroom!* At lunch I would order a milkshake and a cheeseburger at whatever fast-food place I fancied, sitting in the window and watching people walk by. Then one afternoon my manager rang me at home to say she was disappointed I wouldn't be working there any more. *I'm sorry*, I said. *Am I being fired?* She seemed confused. *Your father called this afternoon to let me know you quit.* I ran downstairs where my mother was waiting. *It's not safe*, she said. *You, running all over town.*

Eventually we found a candle that Ezra liked. It smelled like firewood. Like a living room on Christmas Day. We took it in turns inhaling deeply, trying to conjure memories neither of us had.

You know you can't burn candles in the cabins, I said, as we left the store.

I did not know that, Ezra replied, and we butted into each other, giggling.

Outside, the sun was drawing in. Late-afternoon light, granular and faded. *What shall we do now?* I asked, feeling giddy.

Let's go see the sea! Ezra shouted, lurching in front of me.

We ambled back past the tall buildings and paved squares, stopping at a liquor store on the way to buy a bottle of vodka wrapped in a brown paper bag. On the way out I noticed Ezra slip a handful of Red Vines from the countertop into his pocket. We walked on, taking it in turns to drink hot gulps of vodka as the light began to dim. Ezra paused at a harbour, horseshoe-shaped, closed off by a thick chain. Symbolic more than intentionally effective. He stepped over it, nearly falling.

Ezra! I exclaimed. The image of Mia appeared in my mind and I quickly dismissed it, stepping over the chain after him.

He was walking the curve of the harbour, lined with boats with names like *Lovely Maud* and *Daddy's Little Girl*, reading out their names with glee. The water looked dark and heavy, moving in undulations. Ezra stood in front of one of the boats, a red and white dinghy. No seats, just an empty hull.

Look at this one, he exclaimed, his eyes shining. *Let's get in. Just for a bit.*

He sat on his heels and dragged the boat towards him, gesturing for me to step inside. I looked around. The harbour was empty and quiet. I stepped gingerly on to the boat and immediately fell forward, nearly hitting my face on the side. I was undeniably drunk. We both were.

Ezra followed me, lunging. We arranged ourselves opposite each other, sitting with our legs outstretched, waiting for the boat to steady. We sat there for a while, not talking, just drinking. The boat rocking to and fro. I was cold but content and I wondered whether this kind of good feeling was sustainable. I remembered watching something on the news, a woman who couldn't stop orgasming, weeping on a hospital bed, saying she just wanted it to stop. And then I thought properly about sex for the second time that day.

Ezra, I said, straightening up. *Do you ever think about sex?*

Ezra drank some more vodka, eyed me sleepily.

Yeah, he said. *Sometimes. Not as often as I used to. Do you?*

Hardly ever. But I was just thinking about it now.

What were you thinking?

I was thinking, I said, *it might be nice.*

Yeah, he said. *I sometimes think that.*

He moved his arms out over his head, his T-shirt riding up, revealing a hair-lined arc of stomach.

When was the last time you had sex? I asked.

Hmmm, he said. *With my ex-girlfriend. Yeah, it would have been the night before I started on the* WA. *She made couscous then we had sex on her sofa. In the morning I kissed her forehead to say goodbye, but I didn't wake her up. She was sleeping so soundly.*

He leaned back on his elbows, long-limbed and pale under the moonlight. I tried to imagine him as a boyfriend, doing boyfriend jobs. Illegally downloading films. Bleeding the radiators. I couldn't picture it at all.

How about you?

My friend Ethan, I admitted. *In the toilet of a hotel bar.*

Really? I've never done anything like that before.

Also, I added, *I was married.*

I didn't know you were married. I appreciated the measured neutrality of his tone. No judgement.

Yeah, I said. *And I really liked him. Or loved him. I guess loved him.*

Ezra rolled over on to his stomach, his feet pressed awkwardly against the side of the boat, his face pointing out to the sea. *Then why did you have sex with your friend?*

I sat up and felt immediately light-headed, the boat rocking from side to side.

I don't know, I said. *It just seemed like a thing to do.*

I clambered on to my knees and crawled towards Ezra. I felt the same self-conscious neediness I used to feel waking up in bed next to my husband, watching television with my husband, waiting for my husband to come home from work. How I would dress it up in pantomime, knowingly cute gestures and put-on voices, because if he ever saw the actual depth of it, he would have been terrified. Ezra rolled belly up, pushed his arm underneath my shoulders, and pulled me closer towards him. When I felt confident enough, I rested my head on his chest. He wrapped his arm around me, heavy and warm, sort of cradling my skull. I thought, this is the best thing ever.

Ezra, I said. *Did I ever tell you about my friend called Anna?*

I felt his breathing steady beneath me.

I don't think so, he replied.

When I was a kid, my parents would never let me have friends to stay, but they let me have Anna over. They said she came from a good family. Whatever that meant. Anyway, she came round one Friday evening. We must have been seventeen. They ordered us a pizza and rented us a film. Dad pretended to sort things out in the garden, watching us through the window. And Mum was making something in the kitchen, checking up on us every half hour or so. But mostly they left us alone.

After the film had finished, we wanted to watch TV but my parents wouldn't have that unless they picked the programme themselves. They chose some show about a charity for abandoned dogs. When it finished, my mum walked into the living room, turned off the TV and said, Bed. *Just like that. Hard and flat, not a question. I tidied up the sofa cushions and everything and Anna followed me upstairs. We slept top to tail. Lying there together in the dark, she asked me if I always did what my mum told me to. Which I did, I guess. I hated being told what to do but I was also pretty good at it.*

The next Monday at school, one of my classmates, a boy I didn't know very well, came up behind me and yelled, BED! *Then a group of girls Anna was friends with did it too. They all shouted* BED *in unison when I walked past. I asked Anna what she had said. She told me I was being too sensitive and that my family was nuts.*

That's horrible, Ezra said. He gave my head a little squeeze.

It's not so bad, I said. *I guess it should have made me more protective of myself or something. More cautious with what I give away. But actually*

I do the opposite. Give people more than they ask for. To get it over with. I stretched my arms out in front of me. My skin felt warm and tight, like I had caught the sun. *I want to go to sleep*, I said.

Me too, Ezra agreed.

I looked up at the sky. It had grown ugly and grey. The boat smelled like motor oil and fish. I could feel all the invisible particles of dust pressing against me, making me tired.

Shall we get a hotel room? I suggested.

Yeah, Ezra said slowly. *That's a good idea.*

He levered himself up and climbed out of the boat, extending his arm towards me. Standing, I felt the weight of my full bladder.

I need the toilet, I said.

Well go, he said. *Just go in the boat. Who cares?*

I staggered to the back of the dinghy, pulled down my jeans to squat. I watched a thin yellow rivulet slice the hull in half. Ezra didn't avert his gaze. Once I was done, he helped me out and led the way.

We walked back the way we had come, cutting through air-conditioned malls, our movements graceless and heavy. Ezra seemed to be leading though neither of us knew where we were going. After a while he stopped in front of a large building, leaning against the glass-panelled doors. *Here*, he said.

OK. I didn't trust myself to say anything else. Inside it was a strange space. A faux library to one side. Small bistro to the other. In front of the reception desk was a seating area strewn with newspapers and glossy magazines. Ezra told me to sit in the lounge while he went up to the front desk, which I did, my head spinning. After a while he came back holding a set of keys attached to a large rectangle of plastic.

I got us a room, he said.

OK, I repeated.

We took the lift, watching our reflections, watery and truncated, in its metallic door. Lurching down a corridor that smelled like fried food and chlorine, we found our room and Ezra unlocked it, standing back to let me inside, slumping against the door frame. The window had been left open so the room felt surprisingly cool and fresh. *This is perfection*, I said, then wondered why I said it.

We deposited ourselves in front of the mini-bar, dragging everything out. Ezra found two glasses in the bathroom, mixed a disgusting cocktail of Coke, mango juice, vodka and gin. I polished off two small bottles of wine. We emptied a packet of M&Ms on to the carpet, eating them straight from the floor. I lay on my back, watched the ceiling spin. Ezra went to the bathroom and I listened to him throw up.

I heard the sound of the shower then a few minutes later Ezra came out wearing a towel wrapped around his waist. I stood up as he walked towards me, and without thinking, I lifted my T-shirt over my head. Ezra began kissing my neck and I made moaning sounds as he unbuttoned my trousers. He moved his fingers inside my underwear, then inside me. He tasted of mouthwash and vomit.

I pushed the towel from his waist and felt his penis hard against me. I crouched to my knees and took him in my mouth. He tripped over a little, regaining his balance, and I started again. In my peripheral vision I caught glimpses of the hair across his stomach, the white flesh at the tops of his thighs. My head pulsed with the threat of later sobriety. He placed his hand on my head, combed through my hair, then pulled me up.

I pushed him gently on to the bed, pulled down my underwear and lowered myself on top of him. He dragged down my bra so it was wrapped around my lower ribcage. He held both of my breasts and stared at me hard. We did that for a while. Then he gestured for me to stand up, turned me around to face the dressing table. He tried to push back inside me, but it was soft and I had to help him, reaching down between my legs. He began thrusting harder, and I noticed the mirror in front of us wobbling slightly. I watched us fuck quite convincingly for about a minute before he went soft again, sighed, and went back to the bathroom.

I sat on the bed and wiped myself with some tissues from a box on the bedside table. They were printed with tiny koalas. Eventually he emerged from the bathroom and I went in, showering myself from the neck down. He was on the bed when I came back through and I lay down next to him, set my head on his chest and let him stroke my hair, but it didn't feel the same as before. He switched on the television, a home-renovation programme. Our newly clean skin pressed against each other. We were wide awake.

After a while I picked my clothes up and went back to the bathroom to dress. I watched my body in-between patches of condensation on the mirror. The heavy pout of my hip bones. The flat planes of my thighs. Before leaving I picked up the towel, planning to hang it on the door, instead pressing it on impulse to my face, breathing in the smell of Ezra and the smell of me, the smell of the mini bottles of shampoo and shower gel, the smell of the hotel bed and everything we did on it. I started crying into the towel and I pressed it against my face harder, my eyes a blur of hot pink and salt white.

When I was done, I splashed myself with cold water, flushed the toilet, then stuffed tissue paper up my sleeve. I rolled up the towel and took it out with me, pushing it to the bottom of my bag when Ezra wasn't looking. He had put his clothes back on too, re-establishing the boundaries of our friendship.

What time is it? I asked.

Ezra pointed at the television, a digital clock on the display.

Ten twenty-three, he replied.

Fuck, I said. *There's somewhere we have to be.*

We took two beers for the road and left the hotel room a total disaster.

The city was much harder to navigate in the dark. I peered down each street we passed, looking for something familiar, but everything was uniform and grey. Eventually, we passed a park I remembered, and I dragged us down the parallel street. We kept walking until I saw the rows of diners, the man waiting outside. He was wearing the same suit, his leather satchel hanging from his shoulder, his newspaper tucked beneath his arm. He was looking around, occasionally checking his watch then shifting his weight to the opposite foot. He seemed extremely uncomfortable. I pulled Ezra into a doorway and pointed.

See that man? I said. Ezra looked vaguely in the right direction. *What man?*

The guy with the newspaper. I arranged to meet him earlier today. I didn't think he'd actually show up.

Ezra held the beer bottle against his chest like it was a small, sick animal he was nursing back to health.

Well we should go over and say hello, he said, *if he's your friend.*

He placed an unusual emphasis on the word but I let it pass. I drained the last of my own beer, warm and flat, before dropping it to the ground and hearing it crack. Ezra did the same, stepped out of the doorway.

OK, I said. *Let's go say hi.*

We crossed the road and moved towards the man. Walking felt impossibly strenuous and I had to concentrate very hard on putting one foot in front of the other. He noticed us when we were halfway down the street. He removed the newspaper from beneath his arm and placed it protectively in front of his torso.

Hello, I said. *You came!* I threw up my arms to demonstrate my surprise and delight. I couldn't say for certain whether I was making fun of him or me.

What the fuck is this? the man said. He looked at me and then at Ezra. Ezra's face was pink and loose. He was holding his body in an extremely awkward shape, his shoulders stooped and his arms held stiffly at his sides.

We arranged to meet, I said. I lifted my shoulder towards my chin. A coquettish gesture, I imagined. *So are we going back to your place?* I started giggling but made myself stop.

The man pointed the paper towards me but didn't move away. I got the feeling that I could still convince him. That he was still making up his mind.

Who's this guy? he demanded.

This, I said grandly, *is Ezra. He's my friend.*

Ezra was struggling to stand up properly and appeared to have only the slightest comprehension of what was happening.

I'm her friend, he said, barely.

Listen, the man said. *I don't know what the fuck this is, but I'm not interested.*

He started walking away.

Hey! Ezra yelled, and the man turned back.

What now?

You arranged to meet her, he said. *And you're being rude.*

Fuck you, the man said. *Freak.*

I watched as Ezra pitched forward, swinging his arm from his side, landing a fist on to the man's cheek. There was a sound at the exact midpoint between wet and dry. The man did not react for what seemed like a long time before he placed his hand, tenderly, to his face. His eyes looked blank and watery, his body suddenly childish and small.

Ezra continued moving towards him, taller than I'd ever fully appreciated, and punched him in the chest. He grabbed his shoulders and shoved them hard, forcing him to the floor. The man held his arms in a criss-cross in front of him, drew up his knees, and said something about a wallet in the front pocket of his bag. Ezra ignored him, instead climbed on top of his chest, and punched him again. This time in the nose, producing a thin stream of blood. Another sickening sound.

I moved to the side to get a better look, and without thinking, I kicked him. Watched my leg extend robotically in front of me, the tip of my toe disappearing into the soft folds of his stomach. It felt like an experiment. I did it again before hearing a group of people at the other end of the street, shouting and moving towards us. I pulled Ezra off the man, who was lying limp and yielding on the ground.

We need to go, I screamed.

We ran back down the street like wild things set free. We ran through the dark shadows of the park, along the big coastal road. I stopped outside an organic grocery store to vomit, my head resting against the window. Ezra rubbed my back in loose circles while retching himself. Finished, I rested on the ground, slumped in front of the shop. Adrenaline coursed through me like electroconvulsive therapy.

We shouldn't mention any of this to Mia, Ezra said, as we regained our breath.

Of course not, I replied. I looked at the arm of my sweatshirt. An M&M mashed into the fabric. A bit of sick on the sleeve. *Come on*, I said. *It's time to go home.*

We stood up and walked on, red-faced and panting. We walked the whole way back to the *WA* in silence. Occasionally it felt like Ezra might say something. Occasionally it felt like I might say something. But the things we wanted to say were fundamentally wordless. The *WA* loomed over us, a large paternal weight. I felt calmer the closer we got.

Ezra turned to me just before we reached the check-in kiosk. *I've had a good day*, he said.

So have I, I replied. *All things considered.*

When I got back to my cabin I found it was locked from the inside. I gave the door a good shove but it still wouldn't open. Sometimes there were cabin inspections for hygiene purposes. Norovirus etc. I wondered whether someone might have locked it while they went about their work. I knocked on the door and readied myself to deliver a telling-off. It swung open and standing at the centre of my room was a man. He was bald and sallow and at least two inches shorter than me. He wore a white shirt and chinos and nothing on his feet.

I'm Brian, he said. *Who are you?*

Sea

I messaged guest services and human resources and the accommodation office. I messaged Keith, wondering whether this was part of the programme. Eventually, I asked Brian, who was sitting on my bed, and he shyly replied that he had complained about his cabin and had been relocated here.

I sat at the foot of my bed. The spider legs of a hangover pulsed beneath my skull. I smelled of alcohol and vomit and desperately needed a shower. I thought about taking Brian up to the boardwalk, getting him a hot dog with mustard, and sending him on his way. But there was something about his manner. He was like a small stone in a garden. Not getting in anybody's way. I told him he could sleep in my cabin and in the morning we would figure something out.

I made him up a bed beside my own. I used some spare bedding draped over pillows and recently laundered tracksuits, anything soft I could find. Brian silently pulled back the empty duvet cover, slotted inside his little nest. He was still wearing all his clothes, his button-down shirt and chinos. He tucked the cover up underneath his chin, stared straight up at the ceiling.

I was normally quite quick to fall asleep, especially when drunk. But for nights when I was unable to sleep, when my thoughts were racing, I had developed a little trick. Instead of thinking about my parents or my future or what happened with my husband, I mentally recited whatever I had learned in my last tutorial. With Brian lying on the floor beside me, I went about this technique, closing my eyes and reciting the script from the module on communicating via body language. I repeated the principles in a mental voice increasing steadily in volume, but I couldn't make myself drown out the knowledge of the small human body beside me. My whole frame felt tense, like I could jolt vertically forward. And I could feel the same stiffness in Brian, a rigidity condensing the air from his side of the room. After staring at the ceiling for a long time, I said aloud, *Brian, are you OK?*

I'm OK, he replied. I heard the pull of sheets against the carpet and a short, soft exhale.

Can I get you anything? I asked.

I don't think so, he said.

I closed my eyes and thought of other things I could recite, mantras I'd learned on time management, golden rules for dealing with difficult customers. Nothing seemed to work. I moved on to my side to face away from Brian, shifting further towards the wall. There was something exceptionally comforting about sleeping next to a wall. A hard and solid surface instead of the precarity of an open drop. I once asked my husband whether we could remove our bed frame and throw it away, sleep with just a mattress on the floor. It seemed to me unreasonable to elect to sleep in a constant state of peril. But he said a mattress on the floor was strange and poor, like something a drug addict would do. So instead I would sleep as close to the centre of the bed as possible, and he would get cross at me for being permanently pressed against him.

Are you sure? I asked Brian again.

I think so, Brian replied. *Actually*, he paused, *I was wondering. If you wouldn't mind. Could you maybe tell me a bit about the ship? I came straight here. I haven't had a chance to look around yet.*

Well, I replied. *What would you like to know?*

I found it hard to describe the *WA*. It felt like an exceptionally long anecdote. The kind of anecdote that has multiple possible entry points, depending on the audience and the amount of time available. I didn't know where to begin and so I just started talking.

I told him about the surf simulator, the ice-skating rink, the outdoor zip-line, the indoor arcade. I told him about the theatres, the full concert orchestra, the synchronized swimming, the comedy club. I told him about the indoor pools, the outdoor pools, the diving pool, the whirlpool. I told him about the restaurants, the street food, the buffets, the fine dining. I told him about the water slide that loops around the top deck, moving in and out of the ship. I told him about the Finnish spa and the infrared sauna and the Alpine shower. I told him about the mixology bar, the piano bar, the Irish pub, the gin joint. I told him about the floating restaurant, how it moves up and down one of the *WA*'s central columns, how you can hop on and off on different floors. I told him about the casino, the mini-golf course, the rock-climbing wall, the basketball courts. I told him about the Alcoholics Anonymous meetings and the Narcotics Anonymous meetings and the Gambling Anonymous meetings and the Overeaters Anonymous meetings. I told him about the Korean bakery and the Hungarian sweet shop and the sourdough pizza parlour and the bionic bar and the fifties canteen and the solarium bistro and the gift shops. I told him about wabi sabi, how everything is coming out of and going into nothingness. And the more I told him about the *WA*, the more necessary sleep seemed.

I can't imagine it, he said, after a while.

And though I had spent five years living on the *WA*, I couldn't imagine it either. Couldn't even begin to.

~~~~

The next morning I woke to an ice-pick headache and to Brian softly snoring on the floor. It took me a second or two to remember. I pulled my tablet from the foot of the bed to see if anyone had responded to my questions. I had one reply, an invitation from guest services to come in for a chat.

I showered in a stupor, my face pressed against the coarse plastic wall. Dry-heaving over the drain. I emerged to find that Brian had tidied away his bedding and was stood uncertainly at the centre of the cabin clutching a folded towel, a toothbrush and a fresh change of clothes. I felt like death.

I have to go, I told him, speaking more slowly than I intended. *I have to find out what to do with you. You just wait here.*

He nodded to confirm his comprehension.

Guest services was located behind the oyster bar. I think Mia had worked there for a while. She said it was boring but that someone was always offering to make you a cup of tea. I hadn't worked in an office for a very long time, not once since I'd joined the *WA*. I hated working in an office. I hated the sorts of conversations you were required to have. At least when working in customer service there was the acknowledgement of artifice in your interactions. In an office you had to pretend even to your colleagues that that's just how you were. Smiling and willing and eager to please. It was exhausting.

I knocked but got no response and so I went straight in. Four workstations around one large, square desk, sectioned off by personal filers and computer screens, all empty.

I'm Ingrid, I said to the empty room, and from behind me a voice replied, *Hello, Ingrid*. A man was standing in the doorway.

Ingrid, the man said again, very close to my face. *So I take it you've had a guest.*

I have, I said. *He's called Brian.*

Right, the man said. *And how is he doing?*

He's doing OK, I said.

The man seemed unconvinced. *He's having a good trip so far?*

I think so.

He's enjoying himself? he insisted. *No complaints?*

Yes and no. But why is he staying in my room? Doesn't he have his own cabin?

Let's find somewhere a little more private, the man said. He took me by the arm and steered me into the corner of the room, a little over a foot from where we had been standing.

Right, the man said. *So you don't know.*

No, I said.

His cabin is not useable at the moment. It's out of order. Which is to say, it has been trashed.

What? I said. *By who?*

Who do you think? the man said. He lifted his hand in front of his face, his pinkie finger only half there.

Oh, I said.

So the main thing we have to do now, the man said, *is to make sure he has a really great trip. And you've been chosen as his host.*

He's staying with me for the whole trip?

Correct, the man said. *And you'll get a few days off your normal rotation to get to know him. To show him around a bit. Think of him as your new best friend. Where has he been sleeping?*

So far it's only been one night, I said. *I just put him on the floor.*

Well don't be afraid to make him more comfortable, the man said. *I'm sure there's room in your bed for the both of you. If you just, you know, huddle in.*

I'm not sure I want to do that, I said.

Well whatever you feel comfortable with. But surely it is about what he wants too?

He stepped back and extended his arm. I walked past him, hovering at the door. The room felt dense with static electricity.

Best of luck, he said. *And you take care of him.*

Back on the boardwalk women were already wearing cocktail dresses, in spite of the hour, brandishing vegetable-garnished drinks. Somewhere, meat was cooking on a grill. Men ten years younger than me played shuffleboard. I could hear the high-heel click of a game of table tennis. It felt like I was at the centre of the universe. I moved through it, skirting around a pile of broken deckchairs, lingering beside bins where I could find them, sometimes gripping their sticky rims with both hands.

~~~~~

I quickly got used to having Brian around. He was quiet. He wouldn't speak to me unless I asked him a question or had not spoken for long enough that he felt obliged to say something. Still, I got a sense of him. He was fastidious and neat. He lined up all his bathroom accessories on the tiny shelf above the basin, placing them very closely together, in order to take up as little space as possible. He had delicate mannerisms, a way of scratching the underside of his belly with the white tips of his fingernails. Tucking his hair away behind his ear, though he had almost no hair to tuck away. He moved slowly, as if underwater. He smelled minty and a little like milk. He would sometimes hum to himself while he slept. I noticed a softening of my voice when speaking to him, and I had to lower my head just a tiny bit to hear whatever it was that he was saying. I came to see him as quite creaturely, this medium-sized animal with whom I was sharing a room.

I spent those first few days showing him around the *WA*. I watched him drip gelato down his chin, the melting confectionary making estuaries across his wrists. I sat beside him as he got red-faced in the Jacuzzis. I took him to the different pizza places. We ate focaccia and mozzarella sticks, mostly without speaking. Sipped painkiller-flavoured spritzers beneath primary-coloured parasols. We'd return to our cabin with round stomachs, hair smelling of burnt wood. I took him shopping one afternoon, sat on the pink-cushioned seats usually reserved for the husbands, as he tried on different cable-knit jumpers, saying *yes, no, yes, yes*.

In the mornings I would fetch him a hot drink, watch him sip it in the thin light. I made up his bed every evening, propped my tablet up against his pillows so he could watch his favourite shows. Watched him giggle and yawn and eventually fall asleep.

Showing Brian around reminded me of when I first joined the *WA*, an atom freshly released into the arena. I remembered the energy moving through me like bubbles in carbonated water. Back then I shared a cabin with three other new recruits. We were all filled with the same vim, elastic bands pulled taut, raring to go. We'd walk around the external decks, staring out at the sea, scarcely able to believe our luck. Back then I found the not-thinking about my husband easy, unlike now, when I found it fucking impossible. The three women I bunked with left after no more than a year. They had families to go back to. Families that knew where they were and who were expecting them home. It was around then I began spending all my time with Ezra and Mia.

How long have you been working on the WA*?* Brian asked, one evening. We were eating ice cream again. We'd gone to the uppermost deck to look for some sunloungers. The upper decks were generally in better condition, but there were still stray pieces of debris, paper plates and napkins, the occasional dropped plastic cup. Groups of well-dressed people sipped Scotch in the yellow light, ignoring the detritus and waiting for macarons fresh from the oven. We found two loungers free on one of the darker patches of the deck. Looking up, I could see a spotlight gone out. We reclined next to each other cautiously and lapped at our cones.

Five years, I said.

Brian pulled down the sleeve of his shirt then dabbed his mouth with fabric from inside the wrist.

How about you? I asked. *Where do you come from?*

I came from a hotel, Brian replied. *I was staying in a hotel for a few days before I boarded the* WA. *My daughter rang me every day to ask what I'd been doing. I'd tell her about all the things I'd seen, all the food I'd eaten. Most of the time it wasn't true. I'd just sat in my room ordering room service.*

Why did you lie?

I felt a little disappointed. I thought he knew better.

143

I had to tell her something, he replied.

Brian wiped one of his hands against his cargo shorts. I looked over at his other hand, the ice cream dripping everywhere. I took the cone from him and disposed of it in a bin. I found some paper towels and wiped down his palms. *What a mess*, I said.

~~~~

Though I enjoyed spending time with Brian I was soon ready to get back to work. I'd stopped shaving my legs, had washed my hair only once that week. And I was always tired, always thinking of Brian and forgetting about myself. One evening after I had put him to bed I realized I hadn't eaten anything since the previous day's lunch. I thought about popping out, bringing back something bland and soft, something that wouldn't crunch or smell or wake him. But when I saw his face, his skin waxen and heavy, hanging towards the floor, I knew I could not.

I knew I had to make arrangements for him. Had to make sure he knew how to use his tablet, find his way around the ship. Who to call in case of an emergency. The morning I went back I laid him out something to wear.

Baby, Rosa exclaimed when I walked in. *Where have you been?*

I have a guest, I said. *I have been entertaining.*

Rosa seemed more relaxed than usual, even a little playful. She seemed glad to have someone to talk to again. The salon was less busy than it had been in a while, and I had the strong feeling it was something to do with Keith. We had long gaps between customers in which we could drink tea and chat. She asked me lots of questions about my Land Leave, most of which I evaded, and even insisted I sit down for a footbath when I told her about Brian.

At first it was pleasant to slow down, but as the days rolled on, I began missing the former density of the salon hours. The absence of work made the spaces more glaring, like moving pieces of furniture out of a room and finding the floor beneath them is filthy. Thoughts of my husband kept coming back. Our living room, the perfect rectangle of it, hovered in front of my eyes like a floater. The sea-green sofa. The television. During breaks I would suddenly stand up, nearly knocking over the tea in front of me, searching the white walls of the salon for something to do, something to take my mind off things, but there was nothing. *Let's reorganize the varnishes*, I would say. *How about deep-cleaning the brushes.* Rosa would smile indulgently at me and continue flicking through her magazine. I'd sit back down, try to coax my muscles into softening, gripping my too-hot tea. Often by the time I realized the day was over it was half an hour too late. The salon should have already closed.

Walking back to my cabin, back to Brian, I felt a different kind of tiredness. Not a lack of energy but something else. Something I was carrying around. The corridors felt darker and more narrow. Everywhere smelled like rain. Brian would invariably be sitting at the foot of my bed, looking at something on his tablet, and seeing him still there, gently content and quietly involved, was a continual relief. I'd change out of my uniform in the bathroom, wash my face and look at myself in the mirror. Then I'd go sit next to Brian. *What do we have here?* I would ask.

Sometimes after work we would go out for dinner or to the cinema. Spending time with him was very easy. We could speak comfortably with each other but we were also OK not filling the silence. I had not yet told Mia or Ezra about Brian, in fact I had not been in touch with them at all since he arrived, telling myself he needed me to remain available. Then one morning Mia messaged me, with such easy cheer and total lack of hostility that I found myself agreeing to see her.

I told Brian I would be meeting friends, that he was welcome to spend the evening in the cabin, or to do something else. I recommended a few activities I thought he might enjoy. A cocktail-making class. An open-mic night at the comedy club. He stared at me for a moment and then said he'd just stay in, sitting at the edge of the bed and sulking. *Do you want to come with me?* I asked, when it became clear that I had to.

Yes, he replied, quietly.

We met at the crew mess. I told Brian to find us a table, to try not to be seen. I joined Mia and Ezra in the queue. *Please can you get me two plates*, I told them. *I'll be over there. In the corner.*

Why two? Mia asked.

It's a surprise, I replied.

I went to sit with Brian, who was looking hawkish and afflicted, pressing himself against the wall.

It's OK, I told him. *They're really nice.*

Mia and Ezra came back with plates of Spanish omelette, Goan curry and kimchi.

Who's this? Ezra said, not looking at Brian. Not looking at me either.

This is Brian, I said. *He's a guest. He's staying in my cabin.*

He's not allowed in here, Ezra said. *It's against the rules.*

Well no one's going to find out.

Ezra's right, Mia said. *He shouldn't be here. And why is he living with you?*

She sat down in the seat opposite Brian, who made a nervous attempt to answer.

It's OK, I said, interrupting him. *He's staying in my cabin because he cannot stay in his own. I am taking care of him. We are taking care of each other.*

Ingrid, Mia said, in a low whisper. *Can we talk about this privately?*

Anything you need to say to me, I replied, *you can say in front of Brian.*

~~~~~

A few nights later, Mia messaged asking if we could meet up, just the two of us. *This is my life now*, I replied. *And you have to accept that Brian and I come as a package.*

From then on, whenever I met Ezra and Mia I brought Brian with me. Truthfully, I appreciated the dissonance he brought to our group dynamic. It disguised the awkward atmosphere. Mia kept asking when we would next play Families and I kept deflecting. *After last time?* I would reply, letting the question hang.

I knew what she was trying to do. It was a game for three. The implication was plain. But I didn't want to play Families any more. The whole thing seemed suddenly perverse. I also had the uneasy feeling that she knew what had happened between me and Ezra, and that the game would somehow force that out into the light. She thought I had pushed Ezra into something he didn't want to do, I was convinced of it. And I wasn't sure myself whether that was true.

Looking back, I realized things had been strange between Mia and me ever since I'd joined the programme. She always seemed to have the least generous interpretation of my actions or words. Once I was just a few minutes late meeting her at the staff pool and she told me it was because I no longer respected her time.

On some level, she said, dragging her hand through the water, *you feel whatever you are doing is more meaningful than whatever I am doing.*

Another time, she was complaining about a colleague. A woman named Hannah.

Hannah, I said. *Remind me who Hannah is.*

If you felt this information was important enough to retain, she replied, *you would remember. And I wouldn't have to constantly repeat myself.*

It became very hard to argue with her, defending behaviours I wasn't even aware of. Eventually, I just stopped replying to her messages. When she asked if I wanted to meet up I told her I was busy. And I was.

~~~~~

I finally had another meeting scheduled with Keith. The phrasing of the message suggested it would be one of the last. I did my make-up, wore the usual dress. The neck was sticky. Pulpy curls of lemon loosening from the collar and shedding themselves down my back and the musty smell had returned. Still, it seemed to be my only option, and so I dampened two teabags beneath the tap, squeezed them over my neck and shoulders, then tucked them beneath the straps of my bra. They felt unpleasant against my shoulders but they made me feel fresh again, like a facial treatment at a spa.

Outside Keith's office I did not have to wait long. I tilted my chin up at the receptionist as though we were on familiar but ultimately unequal terms. When she told me I could go through I didn't look at her. Her permission was a formality, something I basically already knew. As I turned my back on her it occurred to me I actually slightly hated her and would feel considerably more at ease if she simply did not exist. It was good to make peace with these realizations.

There she is, Keith said.

Here I am, I replied, cautiously.

Sit yourself down, Keith said. I wondered for the first time ever where his accent was from. It sounded like a Hollywood actor doing an accent. Broad and indefinite.

I'm making matcha, he said, tilting a medium-sized wooden bowl towards me, revealing its pea-soup-like contents. *Matcha is highly caffeinated. Did you know that?*

I did not, I replied.

Well it is.

OK. I made a mental note to sound more agreeable.

When you make matcha you make it from the whole plant, he continued. *You see what I'm saying. It's not like tea or coffee where water travels through the plant and the caffeine just infuses it.*

OK, I said. Again.

You grind up the whole plant.

Ah, I replied.

Keith moved the matcha around the bowl, tilting it back towards me. It looked heavy and powdery, and smelled vegetal, bitter. He pushed it forward and gestured for me to drink. I picked up the bowl with both hands and took a long sip, then put it back on the table.

Finish it, he said.

I picked it up again, drinking thick, gelatinous gulps. When I rested the bowl down my mouth felt fluffy and dry. I put my fingers to the corners of my lips and dabbed at them, then reflexively covered my entire mouth with my hand, staring at Keith from across the desk. He had a way of putting me on the back foot without really doing anything. I felt afraid of what I might say. I looked out behind him, the rectangle of sea. It made me think of my old living room, as it usually did. I could remember almost everything about it. Meaningless objects cluttering the space. The stultifying airlessness. The colours and the light. The light that made me feel crazy.

Inspiring, isn't it? Keith gazed affectionately at the matcha bowl. *I can see it's doing you good already.*

Actually I was thinking about my old apartment. From before. Before I joined, I said. *I was trying to remember how it felt, sitting in my living room.*

And how did it feel? he prompted me.

I can't remember, I said, which wasn't true. I could remember exactly.

Why don't we try to remember together.

Sure.

We've done this before, he said. *Go ahead.*

OK, I sighed. *It was a large apartment. I don't know what we filled it with. There were two bedrooms, a living room, a kitchen, a bathroom, a study. All of my memories are of the living room, I barely recall existing in any other place. I remember reading a book. Or drawing a picture. I think drawing a picture. And there was coffee on the table. The coffee was cold but the room was too hot. I couldn't stop yawning. I'm not sure what I was drawing, whether I'd ever drawn anything before.*

Keith nodded. *A good start.*

I closed my eyes, picturing the scene.

It was a big apartment, I said. *It was big but it felt small. There were two bedrooms, a living room, a kitchen, a bathroom, a study. All of my memories are of the living room, I barely recall existing in any other space. I remember one time I was in there and I was drawing a picture and there was coffee on the table. The coffee had gone cold and later I would spill it on the floor. The room was too hot, but I did not open a window. I couldn't stop yawning. I don't remember what I was drawing but I remember getting the urge to draw a lot around that time. Though I think that was the first time I had actually done it. I drew in an old notebook I used for writing down recipes.*

I played the scene back in my mind. Investigated the corners. It felt vivid to me, more vivid than before.

Again, Keith said. *And go further. You know how.*

My old apartment, I said. *There were two bedrooms, a kitchen, a bathroom, a study, a living room. I barely spent time anywhere else. One afternoon I was in there drawing a picture and I remember there was cold coffee on the table. The room was too hot because the window wouldn't open but I could still hear the sounds from outside, traffic and someone playing the kora. The sound of the kora made me want to cry. I was very tired, I suppose. I couldn't stop yawning.*

I remember getting the urge to draw a lot around that time though that was the first time I had actually followed through on it. I picked up an old notebook and pen and wanted to draw something but I didn't know what. I thought about drawing my husband. I thought about drawing my mum. I thought about drawing both of them, crude drawings, of the two of them doing inappropriate things. I don't know why I thought that. Instead, I just doodled my own name, Ingrid. Ingrid. Ingrid. My name felt like an accident I couldn't shake off. I couldn't stop. Each time I wrote it I felt more distanced from myself until eventually the word was entirely emptied of meaning.

My stomach felt heavy and bloated, pinning me to the chair. I exhaled and looked down at my hands. They reminded me of Ezra's hands, balled into fists. My foot in motion. The stranger coughing blood on to the pavement. I forced the thought from my mind and felt the overwhelming urge to ask Keith for a hug. I watched as he leaned back in his chair. After a few seconds he sat up straight to drink what remained of his matcha, tinting the outline of his lips moss green.

What are you thinking about? he said.

I'm not thinking about anything.

I don't think you're telling me the truth, he said.

I imagined tearing magnetic tape from a cassette. Setting pages of a notepad on fire. Collapsing a web browser. Anything I could to erase. *I don't want to talk about it*, I said.

Ingrid, Keith said. *I thought you were going to try to do better.*

Images of that day continued arriving in my mind. Throwing up outside the grocery store. A crate of Jerusalem artichokes just visible behind the window. Drunk and crouched, pissing in the boat in the cold evening air. I wondered whether these were the sorts of things I should tell Keith about. But I knew these were the sorts of things you weren't supposed to tell anyone.

He stood up from behind his desk and moved towards me. The sight of his advancing body both horrified and excited me. I stood up to meet him, my eyes level with his shoulders. Above me, his strange face. I felt drunk, drugged. I felt like I might fall down.

You can tell me, he said.

I realized I hadn't breathed for a long time. Keith placed his hands on my arms. His palms felt padded, like the paws of a dog.

It's OK, he said.

He squeezed and pulled me towards him, his head looming closer. I looked up, saw the white plane of his cheek, his plump little chin underneath it. I didn't think. I just moved my own face towards his, and bit. My mind went to whale blubber, to soft foam packaging. Something squeaked against my teeth, my jaw rigid and locked. My mouth filled with the taste of coins.

He pushed me away, stumbled back, half-sat on his desk. His hand was pressed against his cheek, beneath it a smeared tideline of blood.

I wiped my mouth with my own hand and observed the red streaks it produced. I wasn't sure whether to panic or not.

I'm sorry, I said, my voice shaking. I could still taste blood in my mouth. *I'm sorry.*

I turned and threw open the door and then I was running through reception. I heard Keith behind me, shouting my name, but I didn't dare stop until I was back among the guests.

~~~~~

I couldn't bear the thought of going back to Brian, to my cabin, or to the white walls of the salon. What I wanted was to hang over the railings, to stare out at the sea. The thick oblivion of it. The certain nothing. That was what I wanted. Nothing. I wanted no stimulus, the longest sleep. I longed for the days when my cabin was my own, the hours I had spent staring up at the ceiling, my face pressed against the soft dryness of the duvet. I moved towards the boardwalk, instinctively seeking noise, throwing myself in at the deep end. I often found a kind of stillness there, among the action.

The boardwalk was busiest before lunch. It was a strange and listless time, too early for shopping or to get a treatment. The time had a nomadic quality, guests idling in the outside areas, trailing their hands disconsolately across the surfaces of the pools. Moving between them, I felt lethargy radiate from their bodies, a slow and soupy feeling washing over me too.

A warm wind stirred scraps of litter, occasionally catching a plastic bag, sending it up and out of sight. There were a few food vendors. Someone selling steaming cones of sweetcorn covered in powdered flavouring. Chestnuts roasting in the belly of a scorched metal drum. And there were performers ringed with small crowds. A woman making shapes with a fire-winged baton. A man crafting sculptures out of sand. I paused at both, watching the bovine faces of the guests, trying to lose myself in the obscurity of a crowd. It started to depress me and so I switched to staring only at the floor. I moved on but kept my eyes down, walking like that for a while, and instinctively I began gathering whatever I found in my path, cardboard trays, torn magazine pages, popsicle sticks, as many things as I could hold. When my arms were full I headed up to a higher level. I wanted to feel closer to the sky.

But it was pretty much the same everywhere I went. Slowly moving bodies clothed in light linen fabrics, street performers and food vendors, a merging of scents, sunscreen and cooking oil. The crowd thinned out a little, yielding patches of empty space. The warm wood panelling of the deck with nobody marching across it. I squatted down in one of the empty patches and began placing the pieces of rubbish I'd collected in a circle around me. Soiled napkin. Chewing-gum wrapper. Paper plate. When I'd closed the circle I lay down in the middle of it, rolling on to my side. My knees pulled up beneath my chin, my back curled like an eyelash. The crowd kept moving around me, respecting my space. I closed my eyes, and for an hour or so, I slept.

~~~~~

I received a memo informing me that my tenure at the salon was coming to an end, and my new rotation would begin in a few weeks. I was becoming a lifeguard. I wondered briefly about the move away from manager. Surely a demotion. I wondered whether that was a cause for concern.

I was sent all the usual training material. A throng of video tutorials and folders full of documents to work through before I could begin. I was sad to be leaving the salon but things had slowed down so much that we would often go hours without seeing a single customer. We didn't need two staff there any more. Rosa was also getting frustrated, checking her tablet several times a day. When I told her I was being moved on, I could see something cruel behind her eyes, poised and ready to go, and watched as she held back at the last minute. Later in the day I suggested she apply for the programme, offering to help her with the application. She said she would think about it and, when she thought I couldn't hear, muttered something underneath her breath in her mother tongue.

A few mornings later I came in and found her lying on her back beneath the manicure table, her feet bare, her white plimsolls discarded to the side. I kneeled down to get a better look at her, and she groaned when she saw me.

What are you doing? I asked. *Are you OK?*

I'm fine, she replied. *I'm just bored.*

You should be standing up, I said. *What if we had a customer? What would they say?*

We're not getting any customers, Rosa said. *We don't have a single customer booked in today.*

I stood up and looked at the bookings. We didn't have a single customer due in for the next three days. A few booked in for the following week but that was it. How had I failed to notice this?

Where are they? I said. *Why aren't they coming?*

I had a feeling I was being punished for what had happened with Keith. He had taken away my managership and now he was taking away my customers. He did not want me to be my best self. I paced up and down the small space. The diffuser emitted a thin stream of jasmine and eucalyptus. All the varnishes were lined up in rainbow order. The floor was so immaculately clean you could see your face in it.

Perhaps I could speak to marketing? I said. *Or internal communications? We can still turn this around.*

I sat down next to Rosa's feet and rested my head against one of the table legs. Her toenails were painted alternately yellow and orange. They looked like a fruit tree. *I can fix this,* I added weakly.

There are no customers, Rosa said. *Can't you see what's going on here? Why would they stay?*

I closed my eyes and pictured my walk to work. Cracked glass and fraying carpets. Discarded rubbish that never seemed to get swept up. For a moment I let myself feel how tired I actually was, how tired I had been for years. I opened my eyes again and looked directly at the overhead light, hoping for some transference of energy, to give me something to run on. But only inertia radiated from the white walls of the salon, from all the anodyne spaces of the *WA*. I thought about the gluey music, perennially on a loop. How your body had to fight not to slow down with it. But as I thought about the music I realized none was playing. Instead, white noise was being piped through the speakers. Crunchy, drowsy, formless noise.

I turned to Rosa. *Where is the music?* I said. *Where has it gone?*

Baby, Rosa replied. *The music's not been playing for weeks.*

~~~~~

We sat in the empty salon for the rest of the day and well into the evening. Eventually I gave up and walked home, detouring outside, the salt air numbing and antiseptic. When I left, Rosa was still lying in the dark, staring at nothing. I found my way to the very edge of the ship and leaned against the railings. The sea was oily and dark, promising more than it could offer. I turned inward, away from the water, and let my gaze rest on the scattered guests. A man wearing a toga. A woman in a twinkling flapper dress. And amongst them Brian, definitely Brian, sat in a moulded plastic chair, surrounded by three other men, all of a similar age, all sitting in similar moulded plastic chairs. Drinking and chatting and inexorably having fun.

I considered going over and introducing myself or pulling up a chair and sitting down with them, but thought better of it. Instead I went to the crew mess, something I hadn't done in a long time, piled my plate high with battered slices of fried potato, vine leaves stuffed with rice, paprika-marinated chicken thighs, beetroot-flavoured hummus. I ate everything at a table alone, surrounded by colleagues I didn't recognize. I stared down at my stomach, domed and aching. I went back to my cabin feeling sick, changed into my pyjamas, and got into bed. A few hours later Brian came back. I watched as he rolled up a pair of trousers into a pillow and then covered himself with his wax jacket. I whispered to ask what he'd been up to and he said, *Not much.* He asked me the same and I echoed his reply. The room was filled with stale air and silence. A few minutes later I said goodnight but I could tell he was already sleeping.

~~~~~

My final shift at the salon was uneventful. My lasting memories were of the smell of the chemicals we used to soften gel varnish, the steady glow of the UV light. Rosa and I sat opposite each other at the application table, sipping cups of bitter green tea. As the day neared its end, I stood up to wash our cups, to wipe down the surfaces, though they were spotlessly clean.

Where are you going, baby? Rosa asked.

I'm going to be a lifeguard, I told her.

She plucked a few bottles of nail varnish from the shelves. *My son always liked swimming*, she said. She tilted the bottles on their side to see how much remained. *Looks like I'm in charge now*, she added, smiling.

My new job covered all the pools on board, depending on when and where I was needed. I'd completed three tutorials before starting. Recognizing Hazards in a Swimming Pool. Intervention and Rescue in a Swimming Pool. Swimming Pool Supervision. And then a four-hour video of a swimming pool, during which I had to note down the timings and positions of when a swimmer appeared to either urinate or drown. There were also extensive illustrations on how to cradle the head of an incapacitated swimmer and glide them to the side of the pool. I practised with Brian on the slim stretch of floor space on which he ordinarily slept. He lay belly down, retracting and expanding his limbs, a frog in a pond, and after a little while pretended to flail and choke. I lay down beside him, wrapping my arm beneath and then over his neck, gentle and firm, kicking my legs to take him back to the shore. I was worried about what would happen if I saw a person actually drowning, because I couldn't, still could not, swim.

My first shift was in a small oval pool, in what was termed *The Kids' Zone*. It was sparsely populated, mostly families, toddlers with swollen toddler tummies, mums in large straw hats. It wasn't deep, not even up to the waist on most adults. It had one set of cascading steps and was the same depth throughout. You could probably swim from end to end in five big strokes.

I had a tall lifeguard chair, a red leather seat balanced on top of a kind of stepladder. I wore a T-shirt and shorts. A whistle hung at my clavicle. On my first shift another lifeguard, a blond man named Jonathan, showed me how to use my whistle, what to look out for (urination, primarily), and the best kinds of nuts to stuff in my shorts pockets (salted almonds, dry roasted peanuts, nothing sticky). He also mentioned that everyone called him Johnny.

Johnny stood beside me, allowing me the high seat, like he was indulging a child, giving them a paper crown and calling them the king. He drew my attention to the various sights and sounds I should watch out for.

You see that woman in the bright blue two-piece? he said, pointing towards a middle-aged woman, smoking, in a turquoise bikini. *She's going to ash in the pool.*

Should I stop her? I asked. *What should I say?*

Oh don't stop her, Johnny said. *Poor thing's on holiday. But it's just good to anticipate what people might do. You should start practising that now.*

He stayed with me for half my shift, singling people out and suggesting antisocial behaviours they might engage with. He correctly predicted two identically dressed twin boys getting into a fight, and that fight resulting in the slightly taller twin pushing the slightly shorter twin into the pool. He also predicted a chocolate-studded sphere of vanilla ice cream would topple from its wafer cone and land with a sad splash. But mostly he made incorrect predictions, imagining the worst-possible scenario for everyone swimming or lying down, hats covering their faces, a warming glass of sangria to their side. He explained to me the job was primarily one of intervention, preventing the worst things before they could happen. And to prevent the worst things you had to be able to imagine them. A woman looped her arms through the metal bar, allowed her body to float, rested her head in the water.

Do you see what's right next to her, he said, gesturing towards the small circulation valve, a foot or so away from her. He mimed her getting sucked inside and drowning.

Ma'am, he said, tapping her shoulder. *I'm going to have to ask you to rest on the other side.*

Danger was everywhere and I was naive to think otherwise. This was the job of the lifeguard.

You probably won't get all that many people coming to this pool, he said, nodding at the few parents occupying sunbeds, the children splashing around. *The filter broke a while ago and Keith won't let us fix it. So the water tastes kind of funny.* He paused. *Apparently, he's been coming out to these levels and biting people.*

He's been what? I said.

He's been biting the guests, Johnny repeated. *Haven't you heard?* He raised his shoulders towards his ears. What are you going to do?

He left me on the high chair, eyes darting from child to elderly couple to lone pot-bellied man, anticipating disasters. But all I could think about was Keith and the ideas I had given him. The more I thought about it, the more I could not deny being at least a little bit pleased. He was not angry with me, how could he be? I was his muse.

As the afternoon wore on, people left their loungers and vacated the pool, went back to their cabins to spritz themselves with tax-free perfumes. To don suits and floor-length dresses. To drop their children off at nightcare, sip cocktails and stuff themselves. I was impressed by the guests who remained despite the day's shifting centre of gravity, their oblivious commitment to having a nice time. At the end of my shift I dragged a butterfly net across the water's surface, collecting the disintegrating serviettes. The pool was filthy, foul, and removing the stray pieces of debris made little difference. But I understood that was how it was supposed to be.

I pulled a plastic sheet across the pool like I was tucking it in for bed. I went back to my own cabin, where I would tend to and eventually tuck in Brian, waking up before sunrise to start my next shift. It was nice moving with the natural rhythms of night and day, darkness and light. I felt like I had more time. It was a good rotation and I was grateful.

~~~~~

Each of the pools on board had their own character and idiosyncrasies. The indoor pools had a rainforest climate and chemical smell. The outdoor pools left my calves and forearms pink with heat rash, my skin salty and tight. There was a pool lined with statues of Nordic and Roman gods. A pool in which classical music was piped beneath the water's surface. A pool in which the water was dyed and scented according to the season, pumpkin-spice during autumn, mulled wine for Christmas. My days were spent watching and intervening, asking teenage girls if they wouldn't mind taking their hands from the top of their sister's head beneath the water, politely encouraging men to not remove their swimming shorts. It was demanding work, paying attention, and periodically I would have to retreat to the changing rooms to slap myself hard in the face.

After work was easier. Brian was growing hugely in confidence. He had a good circle of friends and they would take themselves out on day trips when the *WA* docked. He would come back red-faced and giggly, full of beans and unable to sleep. From time to time, on the nights he was away, I would drop by Keith's office. Sometimes he was in, mostly he was not. I would have one drink with him then leave. We never spoke about the bite but sometimes he would touch his cheek, almost unconsciously, as he spoke.

One night after work, as I was eating instant noodles and half-watching *Frasier*, my tablet pinged. Brian was out with his friends, pizza and the cinema. I set aside my dinner, spilling noodle water and leaving an oily brown stain on the sheets. I'd been granted my third, and final, Land Leave entitlement of the year.

I set my tablet down on the duvet. I didn't feel the usual mixture of excitement and dread. Rather, I felt a little weary at the thought. What would I do with my time on land that I hadn't already done? What was the point? I thought about a conversation I once had with my husband about football. *But it never ends*, I'd said to him while he lay on his side, horizontal across the couch. *A win or loss will never be definitive, it's just a temporary state.*

You don't understand, he replied. *That's the beauty.*

I think there should be an end point, I said. *When the football stops. And whoever won last, they're the winner. They're the real winner.*

You idiot, he replied, jumping up from the couch and chasing me around the living room. Tickling me. *The real winner of football!* He said it in a silly voice, a haughty posh voice. *Look at me, the real winner of football! Idiot.* He'd grabbed me from behind, picking me up as I doubled over, breathless from laughing. I supposed we'd had some happy moments, but I couldn't remember most of them.

The more I contemplated Land Leave the more I worried about what Brian might do while I was away. I realized once again that his existence meant adjusting my behaviour. I couldn't just live as I had. I couldn't go out and get blind drunk. I had responsibilities. I lay in bed worrying until Brian came back. I got out of bed as I heard the door open, waiting for him in the narrow space outside the bathroom. I hugged him and he hugged me back, not asking why, just meeting me with the same amount of pressure.

I've got Land Leave, I told him. *I'll be going on land next week. It's just one day. I don't have to go if you don't want me to.*
That's OK, Brian said. *We'll be all right.*

~~~~~

The night before we docked, half a human torso arrived at my cabin. It had no arms, a hinged throat and jaw, and came with a packet of antibacterial wet wipes. I placed it down and showed Brian how to tilt back the chin to open up the airway. I showed him how to cover the rubber mouth with his own. How to breathe into it, how many times to breathe, and how long to leave between breaths. I showed him how to lace his fingers together, where to position them over the spring-activated ribcage. The right pressure to administer and how many times to press down. *Beat. Beat. Beat*, I said to him. *Use the heels of your palm like a heartbeat.* I showed him how to save a life.

After, we sat exhausted across the bed, widthways, eating pistachios, throwing the shells at the mannequin still lying on the floor. I could taste the rubber mouth on my lips, its sweet, popcorn flavour.

You're not yourself, Brian said. *You haven't been for a while.*
I am myself, I said. *Who else would I be?*

Brian fished half a pistachio shell out of his mouth. A little canoe slick with spit, moored in the centre of his hand.

I like to suck the salt off the shells, Brian said. *You try it.*

I prised open a pistachio, threw half the shell to the floor, slipped the other half between my lips. It was very salty. I sucked it until no flavour remained, then, forgetting myself, spat it straight out from my mouth. Brian laughed then spat out a shell himself. We continued sucking shells and spitting them directly to the floor until all the nuts had gone. Then I popped out to the crew mess and brought Brian back a more balanced meal, chicken soup, bread roll, handful of pickles. I wrapped the duvet around my shoulders like a cloak as I watched him eat, listening to the small, squeaky sounds he made as he sipped his soup. When he was finished I cleared everything away and we watched television for a little while, hopping, not unpleasantly, from channel to channel. When my eyes got tired I told Brian I wanted to go to sleep. He didn't protest, went to brush his teeth, lay down on the floor in his nest. I turned the light off.

Don't worry, I said. *Ezra will be here before you wake up.*

OK, he said, sleepily. *I'm going to miss you.*

I'm going to miss you too, I replied.

Land

I'd slept fitfully and could still feel the too-pinkness of my eyes hot beneath my eyelids. I watched my colleagues sluggishly disembarking ahead of me, the slow pace of their movements. I found myself feeling annoyed by them, their ill-fitted *WA* tracksuits, stained and mordantly out of place. I was also wearing my *WA* tracksuit and so my disdain was completely irrational but of course I already knew that. There was a strange sharpness to the coastal smell and it gave me an ache at the base of my neck. There was something else too. I carried on moving across the inclined concrete, a tugging at the back of my calves.

They made us queue at the immigration desk, even though we were just there for the day. I held on to my passport, which was grubby but intact. A woman in uniform beckoned me forward, pressed the tiny booklet down to scan.

What are you here for? she asked.

I am here on a little trip, I replied.

She handed me my passport, gestured for me to move along.

Go on, she said. *It's good to have you back.*

Outside, it felt like I was nowhere near the coast. The air smelled not of fish but of gravel. The only sounds I could hear were cars, no gulls. The space felt almost self-consciously landlocked, a city purposefully hemmed in. There was something comforting about that, though my body still wanted to sway.

I took a deep breath and thought, ah, pollution! I walked down a long road lined with concrete-clad buildings with random panels of coloured glass. I walked for a long time, the sun warm on my skin in a slightly unusual way. A kind of chemical warmth. The brightness lit up all the pavements and their corners and they were all disgusting. There was spit on the ground. Large, yellowing gobs of it. There were grey islands of chewing gum and flattened cigarette stubs. What is this place? I wondered, taking in the red and white signage, the way its people moved, hunched over and hunted. The realization was slow, the piano build in a horror film, the babysitter creeping up the stairs instead of running out the front door. The call is coming from inside the house. Oh yes, I thought, dagger-sharp. I'm home.

I had not been home for five years. My first thought was that that person would be unrecognizable to me now, she would be a stranger. But it was followed swiftly by a second thought, no, she is nothing like a stranger, she was exactly as she is now. The thought sat heavily in my stomach.

When I was young, every decision I made felt flimsy. I would start a new job and suddenly find myself on the wrong bus, heading towards a job I had quit months earlier. I would move home, and then, at the bank, give out my old postcode. The pressure of keeping track of it all was impossible. The responsibility of getting it right, day after day, minute after minute. How was anyone supposed to be alive? The answer presented itself to me, a red and white sign. They drink.

This was where I had started. It began as a whim, walking home from the Tube I passed a pub tucked into the low corner of a building, the facade leaning out over a slab of pavement. It was something about the contour of the brickwork. If the building had ended in a sharp point I wouldn't have gone inside, but the curve made it feel soft, somewhere a child might play. And I was in great need of softness. I paused at the door, the promising smell of alcohol, the comforting change in temperature, the bamboo-coloured light. I knew I needed to go inside.

I sat at a table alone, folded my work coat over the back of the other chair, placed my bag, umbrella, groceries and laptop at my feet.

I left them there while I ordered a glass of wine. I'd never drunk alone before and it felt exciting. I brought the wine back to my table, holding the glass between my forefinger and thumb, ginger and elegant, and set it down. I wondered whether I was carrying a book. In the end it didn't matter because I drank quickly, in steady sips, spaced evenly apart. The way your hand returns to a packet of crisps, withdrawing one crisp at a time, rhythmic and mundane. No need for any additional entertainment.

When it was finished I returned the glass to the bar and ordered another, bringing it back to my little table, this time clutching it more certainly in the middle, where the stem blooms into a bell, a hemisphere of wine nestled in my fist. I drank the second one a little slower. The pub was not very busy, mostly occupied by men, and no one had noticed me. After that glass I felt drunk but not drunk enough. I went back to the bar and ordered one more. I drained it quickly and easily. It tasted like water. It tasted like nothing.

I was definitely drunk then. I lifted my coat from the seat and wrapped it around me, tying the belt of it around my waist. I reclaimed my belongings, laptop bag balanced on my shoulder, umbrella tucked beneath my arm, groceries in one hand. I had so many things to carry. I walked home. It wasn't a long journey. When I got home I dropped everything and went upstairs to be sick. I hadn't eaten since breakfast, a cream-cheese and smoked-salmon bagel, chewed slowly at my desk. Downstairs my husband shouted for me, asked why I hadn't answered his calls. I shouted back that I wasn't feeling well.

I removed all my clothes in the bathroom and left them in a pile on the floor, crawling naked into bed. I was woken by the sound of something being set down beside me, a cup of mint tea. I drank what I could and then shut my eyes again. I wanted so desperately to go back to sleep, but I couldn't, and I couldn't because I was angry. I was so angry at my husband. Angry at his tenderness. Angry at his care. The alcohol was still in my system but it wasn't enough. I wondered, would it ever be? I must have slept because the next thing I knew I was waking up to the cool dark of the early morning, a plastic washing-up bowl on the floor beside me, my husband's chest rising and falling, the sun's relentless insistence starting up again.

I started dropping into the same pub on the way home from work a couple of times a week, returning home, vomiting, going straight to bed. I told my husband I was having stomach problems and for a while he pretended to believe me. But then I began staying out later and later, coming home with cuts and bruises I couldn't explain, wine stains on my shirt, making his carefully crafted oblivion a joke. I would come home crying, come home to pick a fight. One night I drank so much I could barely see, couldn't make out the usual landmarks of our street. He found me screaming in the street, propped against the neighbours' gate. *I can't see a thing!* I yelled. *I'm blind.*

It's snowing, he explained, scooping me up. *It's just snowing.*

Him picking me up, cleaning me down, putting me to bed. It became routine. The same argument the next morning. Me promising to quit. He started finding me in the pub, asking the bartenders to stop serving me. I found other pubs, pubs I couldn't remember being in, pubs in which I did not feel safe.

Sometimes I would stop for a while, for a month or two, and things would go back to normal. We would sit on the sofa, bathed in the sea-green light. I would watch my husband's face, how tentative his relief was, how it would almost be better if it just broke. Better than witnessing his hope, knowing the devastation was still to come. Soon enough, something would happen, and I would be walking home, and I would think, what I need is a drink.

It was during a period of sobriety that I saw the advert for the *WA*. It was during a period of drinking that I found out I'd got the job. What I did next did not seem unreasonable, leaving a note on the bedspread, taking just a small suitcase, and never coming back. We had found ourselves at a point that was unsustainable, at the end, and we both understood that. I'd always thought the dignified thing would have been for my husband to leave me, but he didn't, and I knew he never would. I had to be the one to leave. It was the most deliberate act of my life.

I looked around to see if there was anything I recognized, but there were just more low grey buildings. I wondered if I knew the neighbourhood. Nothing felt familiar but I suspected that I did. I continued on until I saw a parade of shops, a barber's, a solicitor's, a waxing salon, an Eritrean restaurant, and at the end, a bar I knew I'd been in before. There was no question about whether or not I was going inside, whether or not I was going to drink until I could no longer feel my face. I walked in and ordered two large vodkas on the rocks, my old drink, the one I'd arrived at once I realized I just needed something to do the job. I didn't necessarily need to enjoy it.

I drank the first stood up at the bar and took the second to a seat at the back. Opposite me an old woman cradled a coffee. To my left a man with a skin condition stared at a half-empty cider. The air was thick with inertia. I sipped my vodka. When I'd finished I went back to the bar and ordered two more. The woman walked over to collect a disintegrating newspaper, took it back to her table. I watched with the rapt curiosity of a documentarian. When I returned to the bar a third time they said they wouldn't serve me any more alcohol unless I also ordered something to eat. I pointed at the first thing I saw on the menu. They gave me one more large vodka and five minutes later they brought me out a large plate of ham and bread. I ignored the bread and ate only the ham, folding the wet pink handkerchiefs into my mouth. I finished with a glass of wine, cheap red wine, stored beside the radiator, and actually warm to drink. Then I paid my bill and outside I hailed a cab.

In the cab I threw up. There was an argument about whether the taxi driver would take me to my destination. They agreed after I told them they could charge me anything, they could charge me whatever they saw fit. They deposited me outside my flat, made no attempt to disguise their disgust. I walked straight up to the front door and hammered on it. I didn't think about it for a second. After a few minutes, my husband answered.

~~~~~

The bathroom had been painted oatmeal and there were well-cared-for plants, green fronds spilling over the windowsill, nearly touching the floor. The bathtub and the toilet and the basin hadn't changed, but they were sparkling clean with no patches of mould. The towels were towels I remembered, fresh-smelling and spotless, though well used, thinning and softened to the touch.

My husband wiped me down with a large yellow sponge, the kind of sponge you'd use to wash a car. He squeezed scentless gel on to it and mopped my body like he was wiping a table he had wiped many times before. I propped myself up by holding on to the side of the tiled wall, my legs weakening occasionally beneath me. Once he was done he ran the showerhead across his palm, testing the temperature, then rinsed me down. He wrapped me in two of the fresh-smelling towels, one for my body, one for my head. Then he helped me into a flannel shirt, buttoned me up to my sternum, pulled on a pair of unbranded boxer shorts then tartan pyjama trousers. I asked what he had done with my tracksuit and he told me he had thrown it away.

He took me to the bedroom and encouraged me into the bed. All the time I was looking around, looking for evidence. I told him I would not be able to sleep and he told me I would, and he was right, I did. When I woke up he was waiting for me, sitting at the foot of the bed, loyal as a pet. He told me he would bring me a cup of tea. His voice was measured. He returned with two cups of mint tea, like always, setting one down next to me, the other on his side of the bed. He put his face in his hands but he didn't cry. After a while he said, *Drink your tea, it's getting cold.*

When we first started trying, he told me we shouldn't be drinking coffee because there were links between caffeine and lower fertility.

He ordered us boxes and boxes of herbal teas, experimenting with different flavours, but the only one we really liked was mint. I had plenty of caffeine throughout the day at work, but of course he didn't know that.

I lifted the tea from the bedside table and pressed the hot mug against my cracked lips. It burned the bits which had split. I was working up the courage to ask, to gain confirmation. My mouth was tingling and sore.

Did you have a baby? I said finally. *Do you have a baby?*

He blew on his tea.

No, he said, not looking up.

The relief was so good I wanted to cry out with it.

We sipped our drinks in silence. Once he had finished he wordlessly rose from the bed and went downstairs. I remained lying down for a while longer, still very drunk. Staring at the ceiling, I realized he had repainted there too. The damp spots were no longer where they used to be, the stains had been painted over. I imagined him doing it, covering the floor in old bedsheets, the paint dripping from the roller on to his face. It made me feel very tender.

We'd first met at a bar. It was when I worked in an office, the first office of my life. I was still living at home, with my parents, and doing everything in my power not to. I would go to bars with the women from work. We were all there to meet men. We would sit at high tables, see who was around. We would exchange tips for approaching them, strategies for getting them to talk to us. In the end, my husband approached me. He complimented my dress and asked if I would like to have a drink with him. I told him I would, passing my colleagues at the table, who raised their eyebrows and giggled as I did.

He bought me a glass of white wine. He asked me about my job, told me about his. Then he asked me where I lived and I explained that I still lived with my parents. *Well that's not ideal*, he said, and I agreed, it was not. Later, he took me on dates. Trips to the cinema, evenings in restaurants. He seemed so interested in me and I never really figured out why. My parents asked where I was spending all my time, and I told them I was seeing my girlfriends. After a couple of months, he asked me to move in. We got married a year later. My parents didn't approve, could not forgive my dishonesty. I stopped seeing them after that. I'd been waiting to stop seeing them my whole life.

When I went downstairs I found him sitting on the sofa, the sea-green sofa. He had papers spread out across the coffee table. Catching sight of me he seemed suddenly stern, said, *They're confidential*, but made no attempt to move them or clear them away. I looked around the living room. It was just about the same. I sat on the furthest end of the sofa, pressed against the armrest, unable to come any closer.

What happened to your hand? he asked.

Oh that, I said. *It was something I needed to do.*

Why did you need to do it? He looked like he might cry. *Were you drunk?*

It was for work. Part of my self-improvement, I explained.

He was silent for a long time. *I can't tell whether you're joking or not*, he said. *That's insane.*

No, it isn't, I replied, quietly.

I turned my head to face him. Eventually, he returned my gaze. It suddenly seemed like the most natural thing in the world, to kiss him, and so I did, in the dip below his left eye, right on top of the cheekbone. A spot I had kissed many times before. He didn't react but he didn't stop me.

You're still drunk, he said. *Your breath smells like vodka.*

I'm OK.

I've got vitamin water, he continued. *In the fridge. That used to help.*

I'm not that drunk, I said. *I've been worse.*

True enough, he replied. *True enough.*

He stood up and walked towards the kitchen, and I heard the fridge open, the crackle of plastic wrapping. He came back with a large bottle, twisting open the cap like a waiter might, and handed it to me. The water tasted like sherbet, like Love Hearts. I kept drinking it and I kept thinking about our old life. It made me feel sick. The water made me feel sick. The memories made me feel sick. My husband reached over and squeezed my hand, and I cried, of course I did.

What are you doing here? he asked, after a while. *Why did you come back?*

I wanted to see you, I said.

Ingrid, he said. *Just because you want to see me doesn't mean you can. You can't just turn up after all this time. Because you wanted to see me! What does that even mean?*

I tried to hang on to the feeling of being drunk. To the feeling of things happening around me, incidentally. Not directly to me. I knew I needed to apologize but I could not. I wasn't sure whether this was because I was fundamentally unrepentant or because I felt I did not owe it to him. It was both.

I'm not sorry, I said. *I know that is what you want to hear, but I'm not. I'm just not.*

Then don't say it. He sighed.

We sat holding hands, me still crying, for a little while longer. When I was done he let go and I pressed the nightshirt's sleeve against my face. It was too starched to absorb my tears, they glossed the corners but didn't sink in. I felt a strong urge to tell him everything, to dress it up like a funny story, the kind of story I'd tell him about something that happened in the office, something that happened in the pub. Instead, I tucked my feet beneath his legs, got more comfortable on the sofa. I remembered how cosy it was, how safe-feeling and warm. How when I sat down on it I never wanted to get up again.

I laid my head back on the armrest and started to fall asleep again, but then my husband said something that made me blindingly, incandescently angry.

It wasn't your fault, he said.

What?

Even before the drinking, he said. *We were having no luck. I know you tried your best.*

I pulled my feet from beneath him, stood up and looked around the room. I couldn't stand to be in it, to be back inside the rectangle. I retreated into the kitchen where it was cool and stark, the corners curved like they were bending. I looked for the bin. I thought about crawling inside it.

Then whose fucking fault was it?

I never blamed you. He spoke softly in the direction of my back.

I marched over to the bin and started kicking it, wanting to dent it in, but it was metal so it just moved around. Clattered over on to its side, perfectly intact. I kicked harder but there was no point.

Fuck! I yelled.

He touched his fingertips to my shoulder. *I'm sorry too, you know. I am sorry even if you aren't. But I think you really are. Things just didn't work out like we hoped and you have to forgive yourself for that.*

I don't need your pity! I have a son! I screamed. *He's called Brian!*

He stepped back like he'd been slapped, moving until he was pressed against the wall. He looked like he wanted to be absorbed by it.

I didn't realize, he said, faintly. Turning away, he moved back into the living room. Back into the rectangle. *Please come and sit down?*

He tentatively patted a spot on the sofa and I wished again that he wasn't so accommodating. It occurred to me what an excellent recruit he would make for the *WA*. A resilience bordering on indestructible. I thought about pitching it to him, another way we could try to make things work.

I sat down and breathed deeply, breathing like my life depended on it. My husband switched on the TV. It was a show I did not recognize but I watched it anyway. It felt like nothing had changed and nothing would ever change and we were all just resigned to it and carrying on irrespective. I fell asleep again and when I woke up it was dark. My husband was back at his papers. It was like we had never been apart.

Hello sleepy, he said. He seemed suddenly soft. He would often soften up like that, after an argument. He would be clingy, following me around the flat and hugging me, wanting reassurance I wasn't going anywhere. *How are you?*

I rubbed my right eye, yawned gratuitously.

Hungry, I replied. *I'm hungry.*

Well let's get you something to eat.

He took me up to the spare room where it turned out he had kept all of my clothes. They were vacuum-packed in heavy plastic bags. They were very hard to tear open.

I'm sorry, he said, struggling with one of the bags.

It's OK, I replied, magnanimous.

The brightly coloured clothes spilled everywhere. Sequin-studded dresses and blouses hemmed with lace. I looked at them spread out across the floor, all the textures and shades of a person I used to be. I picked up a rust-orange shirt and a pair of black cotton trousers. I removed the clothes I was wearing, not embarrassed to be naked at all. My new outfit smelled a little musty but fitted fine. I reviewed the effect in the mirror and thought fleetingly of the photography studio on the *WA* where you could dress up like a Victorian or a pirate.

Where are we going for dinner? I asked.

Where would you like to go? he countered.

I told him I would like a pizza. He was delighted. A place had opened nearby, just a short walk from the apartment.

~~~~~

When we got there I was struck by how much it smelled and looked and felt like a real pizza place, not like on the *WA*, where the pizza places were just pretending. The difference was both hard to identify and impossible to ignore.

I like it here, my husband said. *I come here on Saturdays.*

Who did you come here on Saturdays with? I asked innocently,

I don't know, he replied. *Dates.* He looked towards the floor.

Oh, I said.

Oh? he echoed, almost defiant.

He handed me the menu, said the Gorgonzola was good. When the waiter came over I ordered as instructed and he asked for a Margherita with extra olives. We both had Cokes and agreed to split a salad. As soon as the pizzas arrived, I started craving a glass of wine.

Tell me to have a glass of wine, I said, experimentally. *Tell me I can have just one glass of wine and nothing else.*

What? he said.

Tell me I am only allowed to drink one glass of wine, I repeated. *And that's what I will do.*

I'm not going to tell you what to do, he said. *Jesus.*

The waiter returned and I ordered a glass of wine, wishing I'd been given a rule. My husband asked for an espresso. We sipped them in silence until he brought up Brian. *What's he like?* he asked, smiling ruefully. I gestured to the waiter for a top-up.

He can be quite quiet, I said. *And shy when you first meet him. But after a while he really opens up. He's been making lots of friends on board. It's strange seeing that happen but I don't want to be controlling. He's sensible and he knows where I am when he needs me.*

I picked up the menu, contemplated dessert.

And your finger? he asked. *You didn't really have to do it for work?*

I'm part of a special programme, I said. *We have to set an example. Everyone on the ship had it done in the end.*

But why?

I gripped the warm stem of my glass, speaking slowly and carefully. *Because everything is coming out of and going into nothingness.*

On the walk home he talked nervously, told me about his patients and his home renovations, the holidays he would like to go on. When we got back to the flat he asked me to stay.

I can't, I said. *I've got Brian.*

Bring him, he said. His voice cracked.

I have Mia and Ezra as well, I said. *They're my friends and they need me too.*

Well bring them as well, he said. *We have enough room. At least for a little while. We'll figure something out.* His voice sounded strained, faltering. *Please?* he added.

Inside, I pulled a few more clothes out of the plastic vacuum bags. My husband packed them up for me in a small suitcase. *Just to tide you over*, he said. He plucked two books from the shelves, paperbacks, and placed them on top of the clothes. I felt like I was going on a holiday. We put the suitcase into the boot of his car and he drove me to the dock. He dropped me off as near to the *WA* as he was allowed, kissing me goodbye.

OK, I said, before leaving him. *OK.*

Really? he said.

Really, I replied.

At immigration I presented my passport. I was still drunk. The officer was indifferent, sweating lightly.

Did you have a good trip? she asked in a grey monotone.

I had a great trip, I told her.

I walked down the concrete incline, the *WA* just slightly easier to get back to than it was to leave. On board there was an unsettling absence of people where there should have been a surplus. But I relaxed once I was back in my cabin, shutting the door behind me. I reached for my tablet to message Brian. I wrote, *I have the most wonderful news.*

Sea

I slept for a little while, lying on top of my bedcovers, the light still on. I woke an hour or so later, feeling thirsty and sick and generally unwell. Brian was not yet back and I was grateful for the respite.

By the early hours of the morning my hangover had unravelled fully behind my eyes, pounding my heart hard against my chest. The sea was moving in large waves. I was sick twice. Lying beneath my sheets, I passed the time imagining all of the people in my life taking care of me. I imagined my husband pressing a cold compress to my forehead. I imagined Mia tidying up my cabin. I imagined Ezra curled against my back. I even imagined Keith, bringing me a glass of water and telling me he wasn't leaving until it was finished. Finally I imagined Brian, shyly navigating the corridors of the *WA*, looking for something I might like to eat. That's what happened, as you aged. Your children became the parents. The roles were reversed. The thought made me feel safe, like there was a plan for the universe.

When I wasn't imagining being taken care of, I vacillated between worry about what trouble Brian was getting into and anger at his failure to let me know where he was. His lack of consideration for my feelings. We needed to discuss our change of plans. I needed to know how he might feel about moving in with me and my husband. Sometime around the early hours of the morning I managed to sleep again, though it was an unpleasant kind of sleep, like eating beyond the point of being full. On waking I was irritated to find he was still not there, his little space on the floor conspicuously empty.

In the bathroom I rinsed out my mouth with water and spat it into the basin, contemplating my face in the mirror. The lines which stretched from the outer corners of my eyes and disappeared into my hairline. I was so good at losing things, I thought. I was fucking spectacular at it. I had to ready myself for work, shutting the toilet seat and sitting on it, switching on the shower and letting the water drench me. I didn't towel-dry myself before putting on my lifeguard uniform, figured the clothes would do the job. Wet. Dry. What difference did it make? I checked my tablet to see which pool I was working at, relieved to find it was indoors. I didn't have to face the fresh air, the sun on my skin, just yet.

I traipsed over via the service corridors. The lower floors were closed for maintenance and the lifts were out of order and so I had to take the stairs. When I arrived, I found that the pool was deserted, the water emitting a vaguely rancid smell. I wondered again about Brian, imagined finding him, rumpled and waiting, in the cabin at the end of my shift. We had so much to catch up on. I might pick up something sweet on my way home, a box of doughnuts or one of those frothy milkshakes he liked, topped with crumbled-up pieces of biscuit. He had such a soft spot for excess. I stared at the water, verdant-green and toxic. Glancing around to make quite sure I was alone, I rested my head against the back of my high chair and let out an extremely long groan.

At the end of my shift I headed straight back to my cabin, forgetting about the doughnuts and milkshake, the crumbled-up pieces of biscuit, but Brian was still not there. I started to panic. I headed out to check all of his favourite spots, the places we had been together, but the more I looked for him, the more worried I became. I searched the speakeasy, the sushi bar, the saunas. I went to all the places that served steak. All the places that served ice cream. I walked up and down the boardwalk, my limbs shaking, grabbing strangers from behind and pulling them around, but I could not find Brian.

Finally it occurred to me to message guest services. Brian might have got in touch with them. I went back to my cabin and wrote them an admittedly long and rambling message. Then I lay on the bed and tried to steady my breathing. It felt like the walls were closing in. I thought about visiting Keith but the last thing I needed was for him to know I had let him down. I only had one person left to ask for help.

I didn't tell Mia I was coming to see her, I just turned up at her cabin. The corridor was hot and dark. The air conditioning didn't seem to be working and every second light was out. I pressed my face against the plastic of her door and imagined myself having a drink, something amber and short, imagined the heat of it moving through my body. Relaxing my muscles and helping me to think straight. I peeled myself away and knocked using the flat of my palm, a dull, wet sound. Everything I did seemed to take on the tenor of desperation. She answered a few seconds later in a thin T-shirt and pants. She seemed distracted, in the middle of something.

What do you want? she asked. The look on her face, at once relief and disgust.

Have you seen Brian?

No, she replied, rolling her eyes. *I haven't seen Brian. Why?*

I have no idea where he is, I said. *When I got back from Land Leave he wasn't in my cabin and I haven't seen him since. Did he say anything? Did he come to you?*

Mia stepped back and gestured for me to step inside. I checked the other three bunks to make sure her room-mates weren't around, then sat on her bed. She sat next to me, hovering a hand over my leg, before resting it tentatively on the knee.

I'm sure it will be OK, she said. *Have you tried guest services?*

Yes, ages ago. No reply.

Listen, she said. *He's probably just gone out for the day. We're still docked. He'll be back before the evening.*

I have something very important to ask him.

Mia paused and looked carefully at me. *What do you need to ask him?*

I saw my husband, I said. *We're going to live with him. Off the WA. On land.*

Your husband? You're married?

I am, I replied, glancing at her timidly.

There was a noise from the bunk opposite, the duvet lumpen and unmade. A foot protruded from the bottom end of it.

You're not wrong, Mia whispered. *We do need to leave. All of us.*

She looked sincere. I noticed a little bag, half-packed, on the floor, at the foot of the bed. I had not expected her to agree with me, to actually want to come. My plan to move back in with my husband had felt like most things on the *WA*, basically pretend. But perhaps this was the real action I needed to take. I imagined the four of us stepping off the ship together, ready to start our new lives. The thought made me feel light-headed.

But things aren't the same, I said. *Between you and me. And Ezra. We're not a family any more.*

Ezra is my family, she said, quietly. *And you are too. If you want to be.*

What about Brian?

Ingrid, he's a guest. He's not real. None of it is real. She paused. *You know.* A slight hardening of her voice. *I've had a difficult time trying to understand. Why you were chosen and I was not.*

I watched her hand, which had moved up unconsciously to grip my thigh. How she committed to a gesture. How I would have placed my own hand on her leg, limp and uncertain. *It's because you're finished*, I said. *You're the final version of yourself. You don't need to change.*

That's not true, she said. She started to speak, stopped herself, started again. *I don't know what I'm doing here any more.*

She reached over and retrieved the remote control. She switched on the TV, began flicking through the channels. I thought about the hotel room I'd been in with Ezra. The large flat-screen fixed to the wall. The small digital display underneath it. The thought made me feel sick with shame.

You know, you've never asked me why I'm here, she said.

You've never asked me, I replied.

I knew you wouldn't want to talk about it. She waited a beat. *So why are you here?*

I don't want to talk about it, I said.

Mia continued flicking through the channels. I stared at the screen, tried to lose myself in the passing images.

How about you? I asked.

Well now I don't want to talk about it either, she replied, mimicking me childishly.

I stood up and turned to face her, pulling her to her feet. We looked at each other for a few seconds. Two stone cherubs spitting at each other from either side of an ornamental fountain. Some relationships are built on a pivot, I thought, dependent on an imbalance of weight. These days we felt increasingly like equals. I wondered what our friendship could look like going forward. She reached for my arms and held them tight.

I love you, she said.

I love you too, I replied, really meaning it. *I'll always love you.*

Good. She squeezed me a little tighter. *But Ingrid. The bottom decks are already flooded. Everything is closing. We need to get off. We need to leave tonight.*

OK, I said. *OK. But first, I have to find Brian.*

~~~~~

I walked back to my cabin, working around corridors no longer in use. Did I detect a slight dampness in the air? It was hard to say. Back on my own bed, I lunged for my tablet, opening it up, searching for a message from guest services. They had replied to me an hour earlier.

Brian has disembarked. His stay has come to its end. We trust he had a satisfactory experience.

I let the knowledge percolate for a minute or two, sitting on the edge of my bed. I felt strangely calm, the hazy relief of just knowing.

But when it actually sank in, I jumped up, knocking my tablet to the floor, hurting my knee. I wanted to move around the room, outrun the terrible feeling, but my cabin was too small, and everything would always be in there with me. How did I feel? I thought. I felt like a fish hook had been clipped to my vagina and threaded upwards, coming out of my mouth, pulling me inside out and slapping me on the floor. That's how I felt. Put a bullet through my brain. Brick me into a wall. Throw me over the side. Oblivion, please. I lay face down on the bed and screamed into the mattress. I lay there for a long time. When I could no longer put off using the toilet I got up, my body heavy and damp. I didn't care. I pissed while crying. I crawled back into bed. Lying there, I noticed something. The ship was moving. We were leaving the land behind.

~~~~~

I woke the next morning amazed I had managed to sleep. Out of habit I lifted my tablet from the floor and found it was wet. I leaned over and pressed my hand to the carpet, the little space where Brian used to sleep, now swampy with damp. Somehow, the tablet still seemed to be working. I opened up my messaging app to find just one new message. It was on behalf of Keith, notifying me of my final meeting of the programme.

Congratulations, Ingrid, it said. *And welcome to your graduation.*

~~~~~

By the time I left my cabin, the floor was covered in about an inch of water. I needed to find Ezra and Mia and we needed to make a plan. I went back to Mia's, knocking on her door. Her room-mate answered, a woman I had spoken to only once.

She's not here, she said.

Is she at work? I asked. *Where is she working? I'll go see her there.*

Her brother came, she replied. *Late last night. I think they said they were going to sleep in the theatre, in one of the boxes. They're going to stay there until help arrives.*

Is help arriving? I asked.

I doubt it, she said.

Are you going to leave?

Mia's room-mate shrugged her shoulders.

Maybe.

~~~~~

I wore Mia's fitted black dress, which was at that point disgusting. Still, I couldn't bring myself to wear anything else. On my way I dropped by my favourite swimming pool, an indoor one lined with faux-marble statues. It was empty of people and only half-filled with water. The steam room was no longer producing steam. The sauna was cold. Something smelled rotten.

I walked towards the shallow end of the pool, crouched at its edge, then lowered my calves into the water. It wasn't deep but I felt nervous. You can drown in a bowl of soup, I heard my mother tell me. It was an image that had stayed with me for a very long time. I climbed in fully, wading through the water, semi-translucent and avocado green. It came up to my waist and I had to crouch before it would swallow me completely. A baptism. It was exactly what I needed. I went under a few more times, enjoying the quiet of it, the pressure against my eyes.

Eventually I started to shiver, and only then did I climb out, nearly slipping on the narrow metal stairs. My tights offered no traction against the tiles and so I removed them. I left my shoes behind too, walking away barefoot. I had a sudden memory of a holiday in France, long ago, when I was a child. Walking from the paddling pool to the little parasol-covered tables, the soles of my feet burning on the hot ground. How I'd called to my father, hopping from one foot to another, and he'd come to scoop me up and carry me across to the shade.

Making my way to Keith's office, I navigated through various depths of seawater, watching it trickle down the stairs like an ornamental feature. I emerged on to the boardwalk to find a handful of guests still strewn on sunbeds, covered in paper napkins. One of the water slides was stuffed full of beach towels. A wood-burning oven appeared to be on fire. Two men in tuxedos fought over a plate of oysters, plainly spoiled. I saw someone leaning against an ice-cream kiosk, lapping at handfuls of melted ice cream. It was Zach.

What are you doing? I called over.

What does it look like I'm doing? he snapped.

It's my graduation day, I said. *From the programme.*

How wonderful for you, he replied.

Indoors, the upper decks were a little drier. Keith's waiting room was deserted. No fruit-flavoured water. No mochi. There was no receptionist's chair behind the desk. No receptionist to tell me what to do.

I looked around the empty space and wondered what I could get away with. What if I removed all my clothes and cried my eyes out? I thought. What if I crawled beneath the desk and refused to come out? Instead I waited patiently on one of the seats, confident Keith would call for me when the time was right. My dress soaked the seat fabric. Water pooled at my feet. After a while Keith's door flew open and he stepped out of it, striding into the centre of the room before noticing me. He was also barefoot, his feet filthy. On his cheek the perfect oval of reddish indentations. A silent scream.

Ingrid, he said. *There you are.*

He was wearing a kimono, jeans rolled up. I'd never seen him in a kimono before. He gestured towards himself.

Ceremonial, he said. *Come in.*

I followed him into the office and watched as he began pacing around, gathering pieces of paper from the shelves and layering them across his desk with no discernible logic. I watched him do this and for the first time it dawned on me that he was either very stupid or very dangerous or both.

So what brings you here? he asked, apparently remembering I existed.

Graduation, I replied.

Of course, he said. *Let's get you graduated. You must be very excited!*

I think I am, I said. *I think I must be.*

Wonderful, he murmured.

He pottered over to the sideboard and brought back a teapot, two cups, and a paper bowl of what appeared to be instant ramen. He set the teapot down reverently, then placed one cup in front of me, one cup in front of himself, and the freeze-dried noodles to the side.

We have no hot water, he said. *And so cold water will have to do.*

He poured tea into both cups and held his out in the air. I lifted up my own, copying him, and he touched the rim of his cup to mine. It made a little clink. He gulped back the tea and poured himself some more. I drank only a bit. It did not taste like tea. It tasted like cold, slightly dirty water. He reached for the instant ramen, broke it in half and offered me a chunk, which I accepted, chewing on it drily.

Congratulations, he said. *You are officially graduated.*

Thank you, I said. *Thank you very much.*

You're welcome. You can go now.

He gestured for me to leave. I stood up and turned away from him, walking slowly, carefully, towards the door. It was over, I thought. What would I do now? I looked around Keith's office, felt my damp feet press into the floor. It was so dry up here. The walls. The carpet. The furniture. Everything was unquestionably dry.

I stared at the door handle, willed myself to move. I thought about Mia and Ezra, hunched amid velvet curtains, watermelon red and fringed with gold. I thought about Brian out there in the world. I thought about my husband sitting on the sofa. I wondered what he might be doing with himself, whether he would be readying the apartment for my return. I pictured two cups of mint tea, cooling, on separate nightstands. I pictured his face, his indefatigable love.

It was time to leave. Maybe I wouldn't go back to my husband but I would leave. I would bring Ezra and Mia with me and perhaps together we would search for Brian. I imagined us walking arm in arm around a bright city none of us had ever visited before. I turned back to Keith, who was still gathering papers.

What has been the point of all this?

The point of all what?

All this, I repeated. *The* WA. *The procedure. The programme.*

He thought for a while, still sipping his tea.

It has been to get you ready, he said.

Ready for what?

Ready for what? he echoed me enthusiastically. *What do you think this has been getting you ready for?*

I looked at Keith, the golden gloss of his beard, the tired lines beneath his eyes. And then I looked past him, staring out through the window. The sea was calm and still, though no less of a threat. A sea-green rectangle. I turned around to look one more time at all of the things in Keith's office, the various broken objects it contained. I imagined all the factories they were produced in. That was something I used to do when I was a child, marvelling at the objects I encountered, the places they must have come from. Everything was so deliberate. Everything was by design. I noticed water had started seeping beneath the door.

I'm ready to be my best self, I said, smiling. *I'm finally ready.*

Great, said Keith, nodding vaguely. *What do you mean?*

I moved closer to the table.

Please, I said. *I'd like you to sit down.*

Keith cocked his head just slightly. *I'm sitting*, he said.

Oh no, I smiled again. *I would like you to take a seat over here.*

He stood up and walked hesitantly towards me.

Good, I said, watching him. *Very good.*

I walked around the large, polished desk and lowered myself into his chair, making myself comfortable. I looked out at him from there, our eyes finally level. I could no longer see the rectangular window, could no longer see the sea. It was like it didn't exist.

Keith, I said. *Can you tell me again about the Japanese aesthetic tradition of wabi sabi?*

Yes, he replied, still uncertain. *Everything is coming out of and going into nothingness.*

I looked at his face, the place where I had bitten him, and noticed tiny pinpricks filled with pus. The wound was infected.

Wonderful, I said. *Now go again. And this time try to add in even more detail.*

Leabharlanna Poiblí Chathair Baile Átha Cliath
Dub...

ACKNOWLEDGEMENTS

Thanks to Hermione Thompson, I truly love working with you, and am learning from you all the time. Thanks to Sarah-Jane Forder for patience and an eagle eye, and Emma Brown for coordinating. Thank you to all the team at Penguin and Hamish Hamilton. I feel so proud to be published by you again.

Thank you to Caolinn Douglas, Emily Bell, Chloe Texier-Rose, Nathalie Ramirez and all the team at Zando for all your enthusiasm and energy, it's been so exciting to be part of the inaugural list. Thank you to Blackie Books and Atlantik/Hoffmann und Campe.

Thanks to Becky Thomas, a wonderful agent and friend.

Thank you to Arts Council England for a Developing Creative Practice grant, which made writing this book possible.

Thank you to Clare O'Mahoney, I will never forget your enormous generosity and friendship. Thank you to Alex Boswell for excellent feedback. Thank you to Danielle Jawando for being the best writer friend ever. Thank you to Jessica Treen for always solid advice. Thank you to Mary and Phil for looking after us so well this year. Thank you to all my lovely friends.

Thank you to my mum, dad, sister and nana for love, encouragement and support.

And thank you to Peet for being the most brilliant dad and partner ever. I love you so much. Thank you, Marek, an absolutely perfect angel.